REFLECTIONS OF DESTINY

BENZON RAY BARBIN

Reflections of Destiny is a work of fiction. Names, characters, places, and incidents either are products of the author's imagination or are used fictitiously. Any resemblance to actual persons, living or dead, events, or locales is entirely coincidental.

Library of Congress Control Number: 2020916332

ISBN 978-1-7354953-1-6 (Trade Paperback)

ISBN 978-1-7354953-0-9 (eBook)

Edited by Sandra N. Smith

Cover illustration © 2020 by Alex Chow

Design by Ryan R. Reyna

VI.I.2

For Benjamin and Corazon Barbin, my parents.

Aperture 01

Artificial waterfalls gushed but their rhythm no longer brought serenity—it sped Enauria's internal clock while the elevator ascended to the platform where the assassin prepared to kill her.

Enauria pulled her blond hair away from a sapphire blade in a translucent sheath slung on her back and closed her eyes for a deep breath. Fear of pain swelled within her heart, but she had to confront and endure the anguish of an attack with the sword she had planted for the assassin. A chime signaled. End of the line. Doors embellished with steel crescents and vines opened. Cool mist brushed Enauria's face and daylight beamed in. On the crystal platform, a forty-three-foot statue of unicorns spiraled in a whirlwind, chasing an indigo-and-ebony dragon at the peak. No sight of the assassin armed with the goddess's sword. Everything happened as designed.

The Seralyn Capitol Tower always had a lofty view of West Scarlet. This time, the scene was different. Fighter jets, ships, and drones crowded the sky and littered it with explosions, but the tower's soundproof windows and enclosures muted the blasts and sonic booms. Despite the battle above the capital, Enauria did not regret starting the war. With tenacity and a straight face, she walked out of the elevator and cleared the ornate doors. The six-foot-tall assassin charged from the left and screamed. Dark, wispy hair dropped in front of one eye and desperation replaced his usual confidence. Enauria drew her sword, refrained from attacking, and the assassin stabbed with an improvised thrust. The blade plunged through her back. She wailed and slashed an upward arc, tearing a bleeding gash across his chest. He shrieked with agony, and they slammed to the cold ground. Enauria lay sideways with the blade jammed through her rib cage, detesting impalement as a step to purge immortality.

"Why'd you say it?" The assassin crawled and grunted, determined to finish the job.

Enauria grimaced and moaned while she reached for the blade with a quivering hand, but her upper arm refused to pull the hilt. With clenched teeth, she concentrated on removing the blade with telekinesis. Nothing occurred. She curled bloody fingers, grasping an imaginary ball to heal the injury with magic. Same result. The sword canceled her powers, and she grinned.

The assassin wrenched the sword out, doing her a favor. Enauria screamed, and he straddled her, forced his bloodstained hands to her neck and muffled her cry. Remnants of fire from scorched clothes irritated her nose. The weight of his body pushed and suffocated her. Pressure from crushing hands made her gag, writhe, and yelp. She thrashed her hands against his arms, face, shoulder blades, tearing his shirt, waiting for the effect of the sword to lessen.

Without her powers, Enauria fidgeted and imagined being nine. The sunset from her bedroom cast a waning auburn light on her skin before disappearing from the horizon. She loved the slowness of the sunset during childhood, but as an adult, sunsets took place guillotine quick.

A surge of warm energy charged through her body. Enauria huffed at the return of her abilities, made a fist, and whipped a hand open, triggering a shock wave. A vortex of silver lightning blasted the assassin into the air, ensnared, and upheld him. His glassy eyes pleaded for clemency. After destroying his life and provoking his revenge, it was time to persuade him with hope. Enauria conjured a familiar diamond ring on a sable chain around the assailant's neck and teleported him to the next phase.

Aperture 02

Conversation and laughter filled the inherited estate. Among a crowd of black-tie guests, Enauria searched for a candidate named Airin, and found him mingling in the backyard. The disgraced former solider looked more mature with a close-trimmed beard. Standing by a flickering bonfire next to the pool, he was the life of the party at this gala. Petite women surrounded Airin, but he did not have the chiseled features of a playboy. Admiration came because of his wealth and a unique cache of alcohol. Too bad he would die from an accidental fall.

Airin migrated through the mansion perfumed with lavender incense, chatting with guests and getting them drunk while Enauria weaved through the crowd and lurked in the distance. Nothing about the atmosphere impressed except the smell of catered food, which Enauria resisted. She came from a wealthy family, and growing up as an heiress, had seen her share of official functions and parties. Two childhood regrets from the gatherings she attended were being an only child, often among a sea of adults, and having to adhere to proper etiquette. As Airin went downstairs to an underground wine cellar, Enauria sneaked in behind him. Psyched to get a commitment, she secured the door. A chandelier illuminated stone walls and maroon shelves, which held hundreds of bottles. Airin selected a red wine from his collection.

No wine for you tonight, Enauria thought, locking her gaze on Airin's face.

The bottle slipped from Airin's hand. He cursed when it shattered, and crouched to pick up the mess. "This was one hundred forty years old."

"I've got something better."

Airin looked at Enauria. "You startled me. The party's upstairs. You're not supposed to be here."

She ignored him and continued. "There's a sword in your music chamber that is more impressive."

"This is my house, and I know everything here. I've accounted for my swords." Airin stood and nudged the cork of the bottle with the tip of his polished shoe.

"It's hidden underneath the stage." Enauria sashayed toward him. "I want to offer you something for the sword since it's on your property."

"It's my birthday. I have everything I want. If there's a sword, I'll break through the floorboards and get it."

"Enchantments protect the sword. You'll never get it without me."

"Magic. I don't believe that."

Enauria held back a smile. "I love changing the mind of a nonbeliever."

An earthquake rattled the wine racks and the clinking of bottles escalated. Airin worried about damage to the collection but froze, experiencing a dream or someone else's memory. People in the vision wore fancy medieval clothing and occupied the music chamber. Musicians played on a marmalade-colored stage. Spotlights shone over a grand piano. An audience applauded once the song finished. The vision shifted. Someone placed the sword in a tear of light, which opened a gate to a parallel world. Airin shuddered and his skin erupted in a cold sweat. The woman had to stop. As a scare tactic, he drew a gun from a shoulder holster under his suit jacket.

Guns annoyed Enauria because disarming gun wielders was a chore. "The sword is ancient. I'll give you exoneration and a legacy if you retrieve it for me."

Airin holstered the weapon.

Intrigued by the red wine bottles and their vintages, Enauria walked across the cellar. "Nations don't revere soldiers who injured a prince."

Airin winced and hid his thumb underneath a fist.

Enauria returned to Airin. "Countries honor heroes. You can be a philanthropist or a national hero with a secure legacy. Three weeks from now, you'll meet a woman. Retrieve the sword with her, together, and take it to the planet Aleria."

"It'll take time to get there."

"Don't worry about time." Enauria chose a bottle of wine and handed it to Airin, who smirked in approval. "Do what I ask, and I'll make sure you're remembered. Forever."

"If I don't?"

Enauria scooped the wine out of his hand. "I recruit someone else."

Aperture 03

The bartender placed a whiskey on the rustic-red counter. Jaye DiVista set aside the ten-ounce tumbler and swiveled the barstool. He needed another distraction from guilt and mourning a commanding officer's death.

Festive smokers and well-mannered alcoholics occupied the hotel lounge, which had a high-class ambiance featuring gunmetal and piano-black walls, dark tables and iron-gray leather seats, and warm pendant lighting. Across the room, a blonde pulled her low ponytail over her shoulder, lowered her upper body to the pool table, laced her fingers around a cue, and tested her stroke. Targeting the nine ball, she took a shot. The cue ball sailed the nine across the black felt in a clean line, dropping it into a corner pocket. The blonde rose from the table with grace and made eye contact.

Pool hustler. The woman stood five foot seven and had the physique of a strong-bodied dancer, flexible and swift. She wore a fitted black dress and matching ballerina flats instead of stilettos. Heels would have complemented her look, but flats made sense if she had to run or do a lot of walking. On the other hand, flats could have been her style or a poor choice in accessorizing. He smirked at her win, and her opponent racked for another game. A loud crack scattered balls across the table when the blonde broke. Jaye studied the match for a weakness, but she missed only for theatrics. After she won again, he faced the bar. "I could take her on."

"Why don't you?" the bartender said.

"Don't want to spoil her streak."

The bartender cackled.

Jaye sipped whiskey, and the evening went on. Poised and in control, the woman beat every challenger. Once Jaye finished his drink, he declined the bartender's offer of a refill. In the mirror, the pool hustler took a bank shot that ricocheted three times and downed another mark.

"Great player. I'd like to buy her a Cognac." Jaye asked the bartender to recommend three favorites and picked the Cognac with the most appealing label. Reaching into his charcoal-gray blazer, he avoided his concealed carry, took out his wallet, and paid for the drink. The bartender thanked him for the tip, and Jaye crossed the lounge toward the exit. Without turning his head, he looked at a tiered, three-part skyscraper before leaving. Arlene was there. Nothing mattered more to Jaye than fixing their relationship and getting Arlene out of a country threatening war.

A server handed Cognac in a tulip glass to Enauria and pointed to show the benefactor. With a smirk, Enauria raised a toast to the man she wanted to spearhead her campaign. She focused on Arlene's darkened room between the staggered amber lighting of the Trifecta Towers. Jaye's love for his ex-girlfriend was going to be easy to exploit.

An eclectic mix of cobalt blue, sunflower, fuchsia, and kiwi lights came through the window from a cluster of low-rise and five ultra-high-rise skyscrapers. The lights dwindled from downtown and cut off near the shoreline. Jaye threw dinner scraps from his takeout rib eye steak and salad into the trash. Returning to his chair, he slid an untouched piece of chocolate cake to Kyle Merkailer, an arm's length away. Kyle was a man a woman would take home for dinner. He should have married, but he believed relationships did not mix with his line of work.

"Precision. Above all else," Jaye said. "We're so precise; killing is effortless. Targets are stats, and I hate it. The last mission was supposed to be easy."

"You felt invincible," Kyle said.

"Overconfidence got to my head, and it hurts like hell. I *almost* saved Lea-Anne."

"Don't blame yourself for your CO's death."

"I don't. The president asked me to command Infinity, and I turned it down. Didn't want to end up like Lea-Anne."

"Afraid of dying on duty?"

"No. I'm afraid of dying unfulfilled."

"You've come to the wrong place." Kyle leaned back and adjusted thin-framed eyeglasses, which he wore for aesthetics.

"There's an imminent threat here." A knock drew Jaye's attention to the condo door. "And I still have work to do."

"It'll be like old times." Kyle patted Jaye on the shoulder and walked across the hall.

While tugging on the strings of his navy Cal Bears hoodie, Jaye wondered how Arlene looked. He missed her smile. He had to earn the right to see it again. Kyle opened the door, and Jaye stood as Kyle invited Arlene inside. Her face was a portal to the past and a gateway to the future. The hallway light added shine to her midnight tresses—and the absence of a ring made her worth pursuing.

Jaye met Kyle and Arlene in the middle of the room, forming a loose triangle to the side of a sofa and a low coffee table. Kyle was unaware the two were in a relationship before. It was going to be fun pretending to meet Arlene for the first time. Kyle introduced Jaye to Arlene, and with a smile, Jaye offered his hand. They shook with a firm, steady grip.

Arlene tilted her head. "I can be a bitch sometimes."

"I thought daughters of presidents—"

"Former," Arlene said.

"Former presidents are supposed to be nice."

"I'm avant-garde. I once punched my dad in the face and got away with it."

Kyle cringed in embarrassment. "Let's bring Jaye up to speed later."

Arlene slapped his shoulder. "Relax, Kyle. I was messing around."

Jaye missed Arlene's mischievousness and wanted to laugh.

One hour later, Jaye paced back and forth in front of a graphite-and-crimson fighter jet. A heavy brushed-steel door opened. Arlene entered the dim, showroom-clean garage and embraced Jaye. Coconut and orchid in Arlene's hair stirred Jaye's nose. He dreamed about standing with Arlene on a beach in summertime. Wind fluttered her silky locks. Sand warmed their bare feet. Songbirds chirped pleasing melodies. The two withdrew from the hug but stayed close to each other. Jaye could not take his eyes off Arlene. Plum eyeshadow with a thin streak of sky-blue eyeliner stood out, like the way she wore it in college.

"I can't believe you left Infinity," Arlene said. "Why couldn't you leave when we were together?"

"I wanted to keep you and the job. I was wrong."

"I wouldn't be here if we stayed together."

"We were younger. We did what was best at the time."

Arlene placed her hands inside her jacket pockets. "When Kyle told me you were coming, I thought it'd be to liberate the country."

"The U.S. won't strike first and incite a war."

"It should've happened already."

Jaye touched Arlene's shoulders with both hands. "The recent chatter—"

"Nonpareil's stateside attack, it's nothing new."

"There'll be a counterattack if it happens. You might get your wish."

"Good." Arlene moved away from Jaye and looked into the portside intake of the plane.

"I want to make sure you're safe."

"They'll only go after military targets. We'll be safe."

"Nothing's safe in a strike zone," Jaye said. "I'd hate for you to be wrong."

Arlene approached, took one of Jaye's fingers, and wrapped it in her hand. "I know you're here for me and I'm thankful. But if you planned to take me home, I'm not leaving. I promised I'd stay."

Jaye clasped his hands over Arlene's cold hand and squeezed it. "I'm sorry about your ex-fiancé. He wouldn't want you to die and neither do I."

Aperture 05

Before sunrise, Enauria set the dossiers of Jaye and Arlene on the kitchen island and took out their death certificates. Both had the same cause of death: "joint effects of thermal and traumatic injuries." She fished for a newspaper clipping from Jaye's folder and read a line circled in bloodred ink: "Trifecta Towers damaged in missile attack." The article and death certificate matched the present calendar date.

"Less than an hour now. I'll catch you."

An alarm blared and water sprayed from fire sprinklers. Jaye jolted in bed and wiped the water out of his eyes. An air strike hit outside the tower, which made getting out first priority. Dashing out of bed, Jaye grabbed his gun, keys, and wallet; put on his shoes; and scrambled out of the room. People filled the hallway and ran toward the elevators. Arlene and Kyle emerged from their nearby rooms. Jaye waved for them to follow, and they sprinted toward the stairs, stopping at the staircase juncture.

"Kyle, the *Delcensia*'s a single-seater. Can you fly it to safety? I'll leave with Arlene."

"You trust me? Fighters aren't my expertise."

"Get some experience. She's in building one, hangar five." Jaye gave Kyle a lusterless, midnight-titanium key and a silver keycard from his wallet.

Kyle split, and the building shook from another nearby bombing run. Frantic people clogged the entrance to the stairwell, pushing and shoving to hurry down the stairs.

"This'll take a long time," Jaye said.

"I can get a two-seater plane."

"Is it far?"

Arlene pointed at the ceiling. "A few floors versus seventy. Your pick."

"Let's go. I'll feel safer with the plane."

The two dashed to a server room several stories above, and Arlene punched in a code to unlock the door. Humidity in the room made Jaye flinch.

At a terminal next to a crystal server tower surrounded by display screens, Arlene worked a keyboard. The lights flickered. "We'll borrow a plane from a resident who's on vacation. I've accessed his garage."

"If it doesn't work?"

"The freight elevator should be empty."

Jaye checked his watch and paced.

Arlene keyed code. "It's ironic. I ran away from my father, my country, my past, to spend the last few years trying to protect what I ran away from."

Jaye stood by Arlene's side. What her father did haunted him.

The keyboard clicks stopped and Arlene froze. "I'm scared of the future. That's why I haven't left. I'll never be my old self again."

"You don't have to. You're fine the way you are."

Arlene looked Jaye in the eye. "I've opened the garage and I'll lead you to it. Once we're airborne, take me anywhere, but not home. My father will want to see me."

"How about Chicago?"

"You're so sentimental, Jaye. I'm not returning to the States."

Jaye broke eye contact.

"Promise me," Arlene said.

Jaye hesitated. "I'm tired of living abroad, but if that's what you want—it's done."

"Thank you. Let's get out of here."

Jaye and Arlene rushed outside, through a hallway and up a stairwell, locking their hands against the banister. When the building shook again, they hugged the wall. The tower stopped swaying, and Jaye told Arlene to keep moving. For someone who hated running, she ran well. On the eighty-seventh floor, Arlene halted in front of the hangar door and caught her breath.

Jaye stood near the windows. "I see the *Delcensia*."

"Are you afraid Kyle will get shot down?" Arlene unlocked the door.

"No. He's a better pilot than he thinks."

Piloting the small craft, Kyle dodged a plane, and Jaye moved closer to the glass, searching for a threat.

An explosion tore the wall of the building away, and the blast threw Arlene, who screamed. Jaye flew into the air and yelped when his back and right shoulder broke his fall. Scrambling to his feet, he shouted Arlene's name. The floors and ceilings collapsed in a butterfly effect, so Jaye lunged at Arlene, grabbed on to her, and they fell through a gaping hole. Fire seared Jaye's skin, and he screamed while debris slammed into his body. A flash of blue light terminated the heat. Weightless in midair, Jaye hunted for the source of the light and flinched when another woman's hand touched his face.

Jet engines hummed. Kyle Merkailer sat on a collapsible seat inside a tank-like medical transport, cupping his chin with a hand and resting his elbow on a knee. Jaye slept on a gurney, and a male doctor in his early fifties sat across from Kyle. "An EMP fried the avionics of one of our missiles and almost killed my friend."

The doctor said, "I'm amazed he has no physical injuries. We'll conduct tests to see if there's any internal or brain damage once we reach the hospital."

Kyle dropped his hand and straightened in his seat. "Search and rescue found Jaye during a first sweep, but not Arlene."

"It's only been a few hours. They're still looking."

"They were together!" Kyle slammed his hand on his knee.

The doctor blinked. "Maybe they had a good reason to separate."

"Jaye said he would leave with her, so I know he'd follow through."

"We'll get more information when he's awake. Temper your expectations in a situation like this. Ms. Asariel might be buried underneath debris, disintegrated from the missile, or thrown into the streets from the impact of the blast. Don't give up hope. Give it time, and let SAR do their jobs."

Arlene gasped as she woke. She touched her face and patted her body. No burns or bruises. She sat in a king-size bed and moved her legs underneath the blankets. "I should be dead."

The semidark room had thin beams breaching the bottoms of thick curtains and a stream of light sneaking through an open doorway to the right. Arlene got out of bed, went to the windows and flung the curtains open. Dusty, jagged mountaintops loomed beneath a powder-blue sky. "Where am I? Did I get captured or rescued?" She pressed her hands against the sunlit glass and tapped on it with her knuckles. The thin pane led nowhere except a steep fall onto a mountainside littered with boulders and smaller rocks. Sighing, Arlene turned her back to the window.

Someone approached from outside the room. Their shoes clapped against a hardwood floor. Arlene's heartbeat increased. The saliva in her mouth dried. Images of interrogation, torture, rape, and death flashed through her mind. Arlene took a heavy breath, licked her lips, and planted her right foot back. PTSD was something she did not want from captivity.

Double doors opened. A bearded man entered the room wearing a pretentious Victorian-era suit, minus the gloves and top hat to cover his short, wavy brown hair. He had an antique pocket watch on a chain, placed in his vest pocket. The man was taller than Jaye, and she suspected he would take her down if she tried to escape.

"Welcome to my home. My name's Airin, and I apologize for barging in. I didn't know you were awake."

"Where am I, and why am I here?"

Airin turned toward the door. "Follow me. I have a story to tell."

"Sure. I'll hear your story." Arlene followed him to a room with a view of a verdant garden: trimmed shrubs, flowers with red and green petals, and a three-tiered fountain with a sparrowlike bird perched on the top.

From the bar, Airin brought two stemless glasses and a bottle of red wine. He invited Arlene to sit at a small table flanked by short, bistro-style chairs. He uncorked the bottle, filled the glasses halfway, and swirled his wine to let it breathe. Arlene snatched the bottle and poured to the top of her glass.

"You're brash," Airin said.

"No, I'm thirsty." She took a heavy drink and stuck out her tongue. "This tastes like bad medicine."

"It's an acquired taste."

Arlene checked the origin of the wine. "Nolticrux, Landen. Is this imported, or am I off-sphere?"

"It's local. You're on the planet Landen."

Arlene sighed.

"Three weeks ago, I met someone who told me the Goddess Aleria forged a sword called the Atrinisy Blade. It's a legendary weapon used to create the planet Aleria," he said.

"I like creation stories," she said in a sarcastic tone.

"I learned the sword's in this house, and that information leaked. Now I'm a hostage in my place. Whoever has done this wants the sword."

"How're you a hostage?"

"Barriers of magic on the walls."

"Seriously?"

"I've learned they confine us to a specific part of the house."

Arlene scoffed. "I can't open the door and walk outside?"

"You're welcome to try." Airin drank.

Arlene stared at the fancy metal doorknob.

"If I don't surrender the sword," Airin said, "it'll be taken by force. I can't fight whoever's responsible for this, so I'm glad you're here."

"How did I get here?"

"Teleported through an energy rift."

"Nice try. You want to pitch me another script idea?"

"I wish I was, because I like acting." Airin swirled the wine in his glass. "Enchantments around the Atrinisy Blade will release it at the hands of only two people. I'd like your help."

Arlene went to the door, opened it, and extended her arm, but her fingers touched a hot, invisible surface. She pulled her hand back and delivered a strong kick. Ripples in the air broadened in the doorway. "What kind of game are you playing here?"

"I've tried everything and I can't get out, so I made a deal with a third party. We retrieve the sword and take it to Aleria. That's how we leave."

Arlene returned to her seat. "Aleria? You kidnap me and expect me to—"

"I didn't kidnap you. What I've told you is the truth. I can't fight these people, get rid of that energy field, or get the sword on my own. We can get out of this mess if we work together."

Everything sounded ridiculous. Was Airin a con artist and treasure hunter who sold stolen relics across different worlds? What about the third party? Why did the sword need to go to Aleria? Arlene stiffened. "That's a lie. You or someone else set the energy field. Don't pawn it off as magic."

Secret Service let the president of the United States enter the windowless hospital room, and Jaye turned off the television. The president's hair sported more gray strands than the last time they met. If he won a second term, the color of ash would replace dark amaretto. After unbuttoning his tailored suit jacket, the president pulled a rolling stool next to the bedside and sat.

"I'm bored," Jaye said. "And sick of all these tests."

"You'll be discharged today."

Jaye sat upright. "Good. Where's the *Delcensia?*"

"Spangdahlem Air Base. I'll have it deployed to you when you're ready."

Jaye gave a thumbs-up.

The president said, "We've eliminated Nonpareil's core military and secured the region. Their regime's finished, but the remnants have taken their agenda off-sphere. I don't want Nonpareil starting an interstellar conflict, so I've sent Infinity to Aleria on standby. Boston, New York, and D.C. suffered a lot of casualties and damage from their attacks, but nothing biochemical or nuclear."

"Anything on Arlene?"

"President Asariel called me, asking if she's alive. I told him we're still searching and that the investigation into her disappearance is ongoing."

Jaye smoothed out a crease in his hospital gown. "If I'm alive, she is too."

"There's a lead on Arlene. An anonymous contact claims to know where she is. I'm appointing you to follow this lead."

"I'm in."

"Kyle will support you. I want you to rendezvous with the contact, investigate, and bring Arlene back."

Pressing his hands into the bed, Jaye said, "I'll find her."

"I'll bring Kyle up to speed, and he'll brief you with the rest of the details. One more thing . . . we got to the crash site from your last mission and found Lea-Anne alive. Her condition's fine, like yours."

"I saw her plane get shot. It burned, and she didn't eject."

The president buttoned his dark blue jacket. "No one can explain it, but the fact that you both survived might be more than a coincidence."

Airin's heart palpitated. Three weeks of sporadic planning and events occurred the way Enauria predicted. Because of this, he wrestled with using force as a last resort. "I'm not a liar." Airin stood from his chair. "I want to show you something that proves I'm telling the truth. It's nearby and we won't be long."

Arlene kept her place.

Airin reached for her hand, but she yanked it away, so he snatched her left wrist and dragged her from the chair.

"What the hell is your problem?" Arlene grunted and freed herself from his clutch, but with a quick move, he shoved her to a wall, pinned her right arm behind her back, and held her left arm up, near her face. The smell of wine lingered on her breath. A knee thrust forced Airin to reel backward. Arlene freed her right arm, charged forward, and punched. The punch tickled Airin's face.

"There isn't time for skepticism." Grabbing Arlene with a powerful jerk, he flung her to the floor, pinned her a second time, and twisted her arm. Arlene let out a loud whimper, and he increased the pressure to keep her from fighting. Resistance halted. After catching his breath, Airin backed away and waited for Enauria to take over.

A glowing sapphire light emanated from Arlene's palm as she clutched her wrist. "Holy shit, what the fuck is going on? What is this?" She panted. With widening eyes, she looked at her hand in disgust and fascination.

"It's called Aura. It's part of your soul." Airin stared at the light.

Arlene flailed her arm. "How do you stop it?" She hyperventilated and bolted from Airin, colliding with chairs and stumbling to the floor. She grabbed her hand. "Make it stop."

"Keep it closed." Airin placed one hand over hers, and the

light was snuffed. "What I did wasn't right, and I didn't mean to hurt you. I'm someone you can trust, but you can't be skeptical."

As Arlene closed her eyes—Enauria stood in the garden, overseeing. *This better be worth it*, Airin thought as he clasped his other hand over Arlene's wrist. "Once we get the sword, another rift will open like the one that brought you here. Help me and I promise you'll be on your way home."

Arlene made eye contact and agreed, which eased Airin's mind. Enauria never gave a contingency plan, and he did not want to repeat his actions with a replacement.

The prismatic remains of an old supernova reminded Jaye of a jellyfish shredded across deep space. "My earliest memory of seeing the stars from space was when I took a trip off-sphere with my parents. I was six. My mom gave me the window seat, and when I saw those colors, I was hooked. The stars have fascinated me since."

Patched in on a heads-up display on the left side of the *Delcensia*'s canopy, Kyle sipped an espresso inside a hotel room. Communications gear was spread across a desk. "Stars are great, but I still like seeing them planet-side. There's more mystery when they're farther away. It makes me think about how people connected to them in the old days."

"The past . . ." Jaye set the autopilot. "Arlene and I have a history. We go back ten years."

"You never mentioned her," Kyle said in surprise.

"We didn't want it on the news."

"I wish you'd told me earlier. I get the need for secrecy with her. This profession's unforgiving for relationships."

"That's why I left Infinity."

"Good choice. I can't imagine being an assassin trying to live a normal life."

"I hope our contact can deliver Arlene."

Kyle gave a close-up on the display. "Cheating death is becoming an art."

Jaye switched to manual control and pushed the throttle for speed. "We broke up six years ago, and it's crazy an attack happened after our reunion. That could be a sign, but I'm not following it. I remember the first time I took Arlene to see the stars from space. She loved it. We were happy and I want that again. If we find her, I want to fix what went wrong and ask her to marry me."

The light changed from natural and vivid to cool and artificial as Jaye went underground, inside an elevator within the Grande Bank of Reveila Sky. Kyle spoke through an earpiece. "The contact chose this location because its clientele is Aleria's richest. Each level has security, but once you go in, there's guaranteed privacy in the vaults. I can't back you up if something goes wrong."

"Understood. I'm going dark." Jaye walked into a metallic-crystal corridor marked with the name *Alteniza*. Safety-deposit boxes were stacked from floor to ceiling. The hum of air-conditioning reverberated in the vault. A chill ran up Jaye's leg. He hated assignments with limited intel, no plan, firearm, or alternate escape routes. If the meeting went sour, he expected a fistfight or running. The bulkhead to an anteroom opened with a loud metallic grinding sound, and Jaye scrunched his toes in his boots as the woman from the hotel bar entered. "Have you been following me?"

She sealed the door and walked toward him. "I wanted to thank you for the Cognac. Not my favorite kind, but I enjoyed it."

"That's close enough."

She stopped four feet away. "Are you afraid of me?"

"Are you Alteniza?"

"Enauria. Alteniza is my family name. I have a title, but I don't think you're interested."

"You were shooting pool last time I saw you. Now we're here." Jaye indicated the room with his hand. "Why do you want the secrecy?"

"This is my family fortune, and I like closed spaces."

"Where's Arlene?"

Enauria touched a safety-deposit box, then grazed several of them with her hand. "Have you heard of the Centerpiece Affair?"

Jaye shook his head.

"It was a plan to find a crystal that controls time." Pacing to the opposite wall, Enauria did not cross the imaginary line drawn for her. "It failed. The people involved used a friend of mine as a scapegoat. They exiled her and went into hiding."

"What does this have to do with Arlene?"

"Everything. It's my responsibility to find the last surviving member. You're not from Aleria. I don't expect you to know how deep the history runs."

Jaye put one hand in his pocket and the other on his hip. "What about Arlene?"

Enauria dusted the sleeve of her shirt to ease out a wrinkle. "I'll guide you to Arlene, but I want you to give a message to your president. Tell him to pursue Garindae in West Scarlet. He'll be there in a few days, searching for one of two pieces of the Crystal I mentioned."

Enauria pitched a stream of silver lightning across the room. Jaye closed his left eye, shielded his face with his arm and turned his body. The lightning did not burn when it hit. Instead, it made Enauria and the corridor of safety-deposit boxes dissolve. Jaye pressed his thumb to his temple and massaged his forehead. Underneath a star-filled sky, he stood on a balcony, covered in shadow. "I feel drunk."

"Don't move."

"Kyle, what the hell?" Jaye looked over his shoulder.

With a sigh, Kyle lowered the gun. "What are you doing here? You wake with the *Delcensia*? Are you trying to surprise me?"

Jaye clutched his head. "No. Didn't wake. I don't understand."

"You're supposed to be here in three days."

"Give me a minute."

"I haven't fixed a meet with the contact yet."

Jaye turned and gave Kyle a baffled stare, then took out his phone, checked the date, and requested to verify Kyle's. "It's three days early. You have nothing on the contact?"

"No." Kyle took his phone back.

"I thought—"

"I'm working on it."

"The contact won't show."

"How do you know?"

Jaye squatted and ran his hands through his wispy obsidian hair. "Because we met and she sent me back in time three days." With determination, he stood. "We need to know everything about her."

Airin said, "I have a theater for music, but now it's a dark maze infested by vines, transformed by magic. Follow me to the stage, but be quiet because the vines react to sound. When we're on the stage, the sword will show, and we have to take it together."

"If we don't?" Arlene asked.

"We'll die."

"You have a strange mansion."

Airin laughed. "A few years ago, my grandparents died, and I inherited the money they left behind. I thought it'd be nice to live as a wealthy person, even for a while. That's why I bought this place. After everything I've gone through, I think I'm at the end of that adventure."

"Not yet. Let's get the sword."

A few minutes later, Airin walked through the large and dark music chamber with Arlene in tow. The only light came from the door leading back to the hall. Vines tore through the walls and ceiling, covering the windows, furniture, and scattering everywhere. The room's stuffiness made Airin sweat. He hated the enchantments revealed by Enauria. As he took a stealth approach toward the stage, he touched the vines with care. The thought of making a mistake and getting killed in his own home did not sit well with him.

As he advanced, he noted each vine's different texture. Some were rigid; others were sticky or smooth. Airin nicked his left hand on a vine with thorns and wiped the blood off with his right thumb. He slowed to avoid tripping, bumping into furniture, or tangling himself in the vines. The vines were smooth around the stage. Airin searched for a crevice. When he found one, he pried open an entryway with both hands and slipped through by lowering his head and angling his body. Inside the dark area, he squatted and pulled on a wall of vines to let Arlene follow. A flash of silver lightning burst from the center of the stage and revealed a series of arched vines forming a half-domed ceiling. Arlene looked at the ceiling and gasped when the ground shook. Vines slithering toward the stage caused a loud rumbling, toppling furniture in the chamber.

The crevice unraveled, along with the ceiling. For a second, Airin assumed the dome would collapse inward, but the vines retracted at an angle. Light crept back into the chamber, and the vines burst through the floorboards and raised a rectangular case before withering to stone.

Arlene ran two fingers down the side of her neck and through her hair, signaling her nervousness.

I'm glad there's light again, Airin thought while running his hands in opposite directions to dust the top of the case. The case had no lock, so he separated the cover and placed it to the side.

Inside the black case was the Atrinisy Blade: a slender, one-handed long sword with a narrow, asymmetrical cross guard and a blade that tapered toward the edge. The sword was free of embellishment, elegant, and aggressive.

Arlene moved closer. "It's real."

Airin flinched when Arlene spoke, and his heartbeat quickened. The room trembled, and he splayed his fingers. "Let's get it at the same time. Ready?"

Arlene made a claw out of her hand.

"Go." Airin grabbed the sword with Arlene for one second. The stone encapsulating the vines vanished and the vines came alive—lashing out, seizing their arms, legs, bodies, and necks. One vine snatched the blade from their grasp. Arlene ripped vines from her body, screaming.

Vines tightened around Airin's ankles and pulled him away from Arlene, but he stretched out for the Atrinisy Blade and shifted his body to counter the tugging force. The hilt slipped from his fingertips as he raked it in. With a grunt, he took a forceful lunge, captured the blade, and swiped several times to dismember the vines and free himself.

Airin's body shook all over, but he rushed to hack the vines away from Arlene. Another wave swarmed, and Airin had no strategic way to attack. He spit and slashed with the Atrinisy Blade in crisscrossing motions, creating a propeller of destruction to cut anything in his path. The vines amassed over the stage, entangling and smothering them. Airin gasped for breath and his vision waned. The chamber darkened, and Arlene whimpered. On the verge of fainting, a flash blinded Airin, and the hall dissolved into a dreamlike light.

Lea-Anne Samantha Claire sat in the middle of five chairs arranged behind a conference table. The seat at her far right was vacant. In front was an empty standing podium. Two large digital clocks were on the wall above the podium. One was for the United States of America, Eastern Standard Time. The other clock was for West Scarlet, the planet Aleria's capital city. Lea-Anne checked her top-of-the-line but not glamorous-looking watch. Four minutes before the meeting.

To pass time, Lea-Anne inspected her Infinity unit. Katherine Cablarenn, a brunette with a mix of straight hair and curled tips, sat to her right. She was an inch taller and looked like an older sister by a few years. Katherine wore black and white attire with suit pants. Lea-Anne disliked pants but wore them if required. She admired how Katherine distinguished herself with pants and open-toed shoes at meetings. With Jaye no longer a part of Infinity, Katherine assumed the honor of best pilot in the group.

A petite woman named Jenna Kesai sat at Lea-Anne's left. People misjudged Jenna as a college student. She had a black designer blouse and a teal vest with a matching, multipattern scarf bought from a thrift store. Her black hair dangled in a bob, and she had rugged shoes for running or hiking. Jenna's off-duty personality was bubbly and convivial. She and Katherine confided in each other. Among the three women, Lea-Anne was the only one who had polished nails.

On the far left sat the six-foot-two Clarence Abigania, the group's tallest member. He was third oldest after Jenna and Katherine, but his face identified him as the most experienced. He looked business savvy in a gray suit with no tie—and wore a wedding ring although he was not married.

Two minutes before the hour, a man wearing a pair of thin-framed eyeglasses entered the room with a style resembling

Katherine's: slim-fit black suit, classic white dress shirt, and a skinny black tie. He sat in the vacant seat without introducing himself. Lea-Anne peered over Katherine to study him, but before she could say anything, President Ryan Del A Cruise entered. The group stood at attention as the president walked to the podium.

"At ease," the president said. "I'd like to introduce you to Kyle Merkailer. He'll be joining Infinity working special reconnaissance. We've learned an affiliate from Nonpareil, Veylen Garindae, has taken several military ships off-sphere. We're still trying to assess how many. In a few minutes, I'll provide you with Garindae's dossier. We believe he's connected to individuals who overthrew the government.

"A source here in Aleria says Garindae is after one of two missing pieces of a crystal that can control time. The UN needs you to stop him from getting it.

"I met with top Alerian officials. They've agreed to share intel with us in a coalition called Fherazin Division. In case you're wondering about the name, Fherazin Venar was a medieval heroine, honored as the 'Savior of Aleria.' It's fitting to continue her legacy of protection in what we do.

"While in this division, you'll still operate under your Infinity call signs, except for your leader."

The president held the sides of the podium. "The objective of Fherazin Division will be to investigate Princess Enauria Alteniza. You'll be briefed on her.

"We want to know if she has any connection to this crystal, or to Garindae. You're to counter her if she proves hostile, but for now, Garindae is your first priority.

"Now I'd like to introduce you to the field lead of Fherazin Division." The president faced the door and his expression marked with admiration. "Jaye DiVista, if you please."

Aperture 13

Lea-Anne read Enauria's dossier.

Princess Enauria Azenith Alteniza. *Wonderful name.* Daughter of Queen Azenith . . . *She has her mother's first name.* Azenith Evrelle Alteniza. *Named her daughter well.* Enauria's birth certificate: *This is calligraphy for a princess. Faded, but the lines have finesse.* Final descendant of a royal lineage whose family governed the island nation Erginar . . . in the year—*that's over six hundred years ago! What the hell?* Father, deceased. Killed during the . . . War. *He died, let's see . . . she was young, too young to remember. The records are inconsistent. Father left? This report says . . . he never returned. Hmmm. No mention of a war. It's inconclusive.* Enauria refused an arranged marriage by her mother. *I feel sorry for women in arranged marriages, if they're powerless. They had no choice but to obey their parents.*

Lea-Anne stopped reading and made eye contact with Jaye, standing behind the podium. *He didn't take Infinity when he had the chance. Now he pulls this stunt. What a bastard.* She lowered her head. *We're talking about this as soon as this is done.* She continued reading.

The cousin of Fherazin Venar. *Fherazin Division. Interesting choice for a name, Mr. President.* Traveled with Fherazin to . . . *She fell from a tower? . . .* but survived. *Was this a short fall? How tall is the tower?* The Olihoricon Tower was—*A fall like that should've killed her.* Recovered from injuries . . . and attended to by Queen Caneria. *She's the famous queen who abandoned her kingdom.* Enauria and Fherazin fought together in the Battle of . . . After the battle, Enauria vanished. There has been no recorded contact with her since. *Oh fuck me.*

Arlene lay on a steel panel floor and woke to the sound of machinery. The compartment had uneven lighting, scorched reds and yellows, mixed with sterling and black. After rising, she shook Airin and pointed at a cluster of vertical piping. "We're on a ship, belowdecks, near the engine room. You were right about the energy rift, but I think we traded one location for another."

Airin grabbed the Atrinisy Blade. It was snazzy, with a natural glow, and would have been a museum piece or something to show off in a private collection. He shifted his grip on the sword and winced when it vanished. Arlene gasped.

"I thought about not holding it, and it went away." Airin had an incredulous look in his eyes.

"That's our only weapon. Where did it go?"

With a shake of his hand, the weapon returned in midair, accompanied by a light gust of cold wind. Airin grasped the handle before the sword fell. "It returns when I focus on it."

She mouthed *wow*.

Airin tested the sword in different positions and stabilized the blade over his hand. "It's well balanced." The sword disappeared and reappeared in rapid succession, and Airin smiled from the swooshing of the air. "Psychic wielding. I like this."

"I hope there aren't side effects."

Airin exhaled. "We'll see."

Arlene stepped closer to a bulkhead and placed a hand on her hip. "I've traveled on several types of ships with my father. I'm familiar with the layouts."

"Did he captain a ship?"

"He was the president of the United States."

"I'm traveling with a presidential daughter."

"Follow my lead and back me up if we get into trouble."

"I look forward to testing this." Airin made the sword vanish.

"Let's gamble." Arlene tied her hair back and opened the bulk-head. Dark floors. Narrow gray corridor. Bright side and overhead lighting. A typical military vessel. They snuck through the lower decks, searching for topside access, but nobody was in sight. Arlene kept checking to see if anyone was nearby. The abandonment of the ship made her restless. "I think we fell into a trap."

Enauria teleported aboard the ship and stood in a passageway. Airin and Arlene crossed the intersection, and she triggered the intrusion alarm from a communication panel on the wall. The ship's crew would have discovered them, but she kick-started the process. There was no reason to see the events unfold, so she teleported away.

Jaye and Kyle got into an elevator and both reached to press the button for the destination floor. With a laugh, Jaye stepped back to let Kyle select. Lea-Anne ran to the elevator in high heels as the doors closed, and Kyle extended his foot to stop them from shutting. If there was anyone who'd mastered running in heels, it was her.

Lea-Anne stood in the threshold. "Merkailer, may I have a private conversation with him?"

"I'll take the stairs." Kyle departed the elevator, turned about-face, and the blank silver doors shut.

Jaye amped himself up for the conversation.

The elevator ascended, but Lea-Anne pressed the hold button. "I'd like to clarify things, off record."

"Off-record, you got it." Jaye waited for Lea-Anne to continue, but when she didn't say anything right away, he spoke up. "Do you know how hard this is? Finding out you're alive? That Ryan kept me in the dark so I could be objective?"

"He wanted you to clear your head."

"I wanted none of this to happen."

Lea-Anne folded her arms across her chest. "You wanted the promotion."

"He offered me your spot—before he knew you were alive."

"I know you were never happy with a demotion."

"Who'd be happy demoted in anything, especially Infinity?"

"You've used this Enauria assignment to get ahead. You had an opportunity, and when you didn't take it, you felt guilty, so you had to pull this."

Jaye flung his hands in the air. He looked at her in amazement. "Is that what you think this is, a power play to get rank over you? No. Del A Cruise appointed me here—"

"You're disillusioned."

"Excuse me?"

Lea-Anne tugged on the left side of her dark gray peacoat. "When you commanded Infinity, you had to do your job and coast. You've lost track of what leadership is about."

"Leadership," Jaye said with sarcasm.

"Del A Cruise put you in charge of Fherazin Division because you have firsthand experience with our enemy, not because you deserve it. If you never met her, he wouldn't have bothered. Your record—"

"It was one time."

"Doesn't matter!" Hair fell across Lea-Anne's lips, and she pulled it away.

"I slipped, one time." Jaye scrunched his toes inside his shoes.

"Listen to yourself. You make it sound so simple. They brought me in to replace you. You should've faced court-martial . . . and been discharged." She flailed her left arm and slammed her hand against her thigh. The skirt of her black dress swayed. "It pisses me off how the president finds new ways to let you slide. I'm supposed to supervise you, but here we are, roles in reversal."

At a chair near the elevator exit, Kyle got a pristine view of West Scarlet's tallest building, the five hundred-year-old Seralyn Vinét Capitol Tower. The structure was luminous at nighttime, by itself, and no other high rise came close to surpassing its height. Legend claimed "Old Magic" protected the tower. Kyle had heard the story growing up on Aleria, and wondered if it only applied to the original tower or included the retrofit.

Jaye emerged from the elevator with a scowl, and Kyle walked with him. "Do you know why they demoted me in Infinity?" Jaye asked.

Kyle kept pace and shook his head. "I didn't look it up. Everyone's entitled to their secrets."

Jaye pointed at a group of empty seats, sat, and draped his arm over the top of the chair. "I made a mistake on a mission a few years back, and Lea-Anne used it as the reason I shouldn't be trusted."

"She's pissed the backup QB got the starting job."

"There was a man named Cozmin, and the Syndicate hired him to refine Permidial Drives. They wanted to take the technology allowing ships to wake"—Jaye gestured with his hands—"and make it small enough to use in planes. The final goal was to miniaturize the tech for teleporting weapons. It's impossible to counter, and the origin of the weapons couldn't be traced."

Jaye crossed his leg. "President Asariel ordered us to take out Cozmin and destroy what he was working on, but I changed the plan after we killed Cozmin." He checked for eavesdroppers. "Remember the stock market crash a few years ago?"

"The Massive Plunge."

"I went after the Syndicate's finances. I thought I could finish them if I stopped their ability to do business."

"Their black market ties to society," Kyle said. "When you hacked the accounts, the meltdown must have gone to the core."

"Arlene's father authorized the hit on Cozmin and a financial officer before he left office. He had to clean the mess. With public backlash and pressure from the UN, he had to strip my command to keep me on board Infinity."

"That's how you got the *Delcensia*. You used the Syndicate's money to commission the plane."

"My trophy of villainy."

Kyle chuckled at the verbal bravado. "Weren't you worried they'd come after you for stealing their design?"

"I had the *Delcensia*'s technical data destroyed after final assembly. If they ever get me, or the plane . . . I'll deal with it when it happens."

"You commissioned an untested, experimental engine that could've killed you if Cozmin got his math wrong. Ever think about that?"

"I'm still here. That's what matters."

A male voice on the PA system interrupted Kyle before he could speak. "Crystal Palace, Alert One. Repeat: Crystal Palace, Alert One. This is not a drill. Attention: Fherazin Division. Priority Scramble. Repeat: Priority Scramble."

Veylen Garindae sat in the cabin of a small, heavy-armor support plane commandeered from his ship. A man dressed in a dirty suit pointed an elegant sword at him, and the woman, who was somewhere in her mid- to late twenties, flew the plane in a peculiar way: aggressive, novice, and desperate.

Garindae bowed his head, folded his hands in his lap, and closed his eyes. Who were these people, and how had they gotten aboard his ship? What had happened to his men? Why did no one detect them? Was getting captured his own fault, or was fate unkind? He glared at the man with the sword and retraced what had happened in his head. The stowaways must have followed him to his quarters. He didn't lock the door, so they took him hostage, stole the plane, and made a clean escape. For now. The woman's inexperience as a pilot would get them killed.

"I don't want to die because of some rookie," Garindae said.

Alarms rang and indicators flashed, clashing with Arlene's concentration as she flew into West Scarlet. "Fuck the instruments. Just fly the plane," Arlene said.

Her hands shook, her heart raced, and sweat formed on her brow and grew heavy on her chest and back as the plane took enemy fire. Arlene pushed the throttle, trying to remember techniques Jaye had taught her about flying. She banked right to avoid friendly fire from anti-air batteries and missile launchers and descended toward the city to fly over the largest of three rivers that cut through downtown.

Missile lock. The tone was different from the symphony of other alarms. A steel suspension bridge drew closer. Arlene dove under it. Her rearview camera showed her a missile explosion collapsing crossbeams. One of the enemy planes sliced through the bridge in a display of aerial acrobatics. A second bridge was upriver. Arlene swerved away from the river, slipping her plane between the margins of skyscrapers. "I won't last long here."

Goose bumps formed on her shaking arms as she raised the elevators of the plane to climb back into open airspace.

Two planes chased Arlene with the aim to rescue Garindae alive. Cannon fire erupted in a series of orange bursts. The pilots continued to fire, attempting to disable the plane.

Garindae grinned because his people were close.

The man in the suit angled the sword in another direction as the plane rocked. "I didn't want to maim or kill you by accident."

"Appreciate that. I like this face the way it is." *If they rescue me, I'll get this asshole with the sword first*, Garindae thought.

An engine gave out and the hull buckled, causing Arlene to jolt. The plane was losing speed and altitude. She did what she could to stabilize it and restarted the engine. "Come on, come on." She checked her instruments. The engine roared back to life, and as soon as power returned, she headed for cover into the city, praying they survived. A burst of light erupted between buildings, and the *Delcensia* volleyed through a vertical hairpin. "Thank God you're here!" Arlene said.

Jaye tracked Arlene's plane and did not blink. "Listen up. Her comms are off, so let's take out the targets and keep her airborne. Lea-Anne, you're with Jenna. I want salvo fire from the rear to interrupt the attack. Clarence, rendezvous with Arlene and take point. Make sure she follows you. Kat, do a sweep and eliminate the remaining enemy jets breaching West Scarlet."

"Jaye, we're bringing them your way," Lea-Anne said.

"Copy." Jaye reached a turning point at the edge of downtown and circled back. Non-reinforced windows exploded, leaving a trail of shattered glass several blocks down. Arlene broke through an intersection right after Clarence. Jaye pursued from the flank, caught his prey off guard, and depressed the trigger. "You can thank me later."

Arlene lay on a leather sofa inside the Crystal Palace. An aquarium near the wall provided the room with a glow. Plants and colorful decorations surrounded fish, which drifted as prisoners of survival. Arlene was in the middle of the room, on a causeway toward the window, where city light met aquarium light, creating vignettes of darkness around furnished spaces. Combat air patrols circled the watchtowers of West Scarlet, and Arlene was glad she could not hear their engines because planes would give her nightmares.

She held the phone to her left ear, tucked underneath her hair, listening to a man she once called dad—others called him Noel, and many others, President Asariel.

"I'm alive because Jaye taught me how to fly." Arlene loosened her shoes one at a time, sat, and flung them off her feet, into the corner.

"I know. You told me that." She looked at the ceiling, ran her hand through her hair, down her neck, and traced her hand across the sofa to collect two items. While supporting the phone with her shoulder, she freed a cigarette from its carton, put it to her lips, and lit it.

She tossed the lighter to the floor and took a drag. "You want to make up time with me?"

The cigarette depleted, and she shook the ashes onto her chest.

"Why couldn't you do this when I was growing up? You missed my graduation."

An alarm went off.

"It's nothing. I said it's nothing! Don't worry about the alarm." Arlene scurried to the bathroom, threw the unfinished cigarette butt into the toilet without flushing it, and looked at herself in the mirror. The image was trash, and she wanted to tear it into pieces.

"Your business came first. Now you want to make up time." She left the bathroom while listening to the argument, paced around the sofa, and ran her hands through her hair. A knock stalled her.

Arlene muted the line and answered the door.

"The smoke alarm went off," a security officer said. "Is everything all right?"

Arlene wiped her forehead with the back of her hand. "Yeah, it's fine."

"You can't smoke inside the Crystal Palace."

"Whatever. I put it out."

The guard switched the radio off and left.

Arlene closed the door, sighed, slumped to the floor with her back against the door, and took her father off hold. "I'm not ready to come back." She breathed into the phone. "You're not the president anymore. Mom's gone, and you have nothing else to do, that's why you want to see me."

More listening. Pleading.

"I met Jaye, and you brought him to Infinity," Arlene cried. "Look at what you did to him . . . and to us. You ruined everything."

She cut her father off when he mentioned her ex-fiancé. "Don't you even say his name!"

Arlene splayed the fingers of her left hand and touched the spot where she had once worn her engagement ring. It was a mistake to sell it. Because she loved Marshall more than Jaye.

"If I *ever* find out who killed him . . ." She slumped farther to the floor and assumed a sleeping position, head on the plush carpet. The volume was loud enough to hear without supporting the phone. "I'm sorry. When we go back to Earth, I don't want to see you. Not yet."

Brokenhearted silence came from the other end of the line.

Then, "Arlene?" her father said. "Arlene, please. I love you."

Arlene cut the line, closed her eyes, and sobbed. The hair covering her face was wet, and her clothes were littered in ashes. She dreamed about living in Europe with Marshall and wished the revolution had never happened.

Jaye drove a gunmetal sedan through the twilight rain of West Scarlet, with Arlene in the passenger seat, her feet on the dashboard. The engine gave a bass-like purr and the rhythmic downpour of the raindrops created a sheen on buildings and the wide, calm streets. "Kyle gave me a crash course on Aleria's history. Magic created the planet, people fought wars with magic, and now magic has disappeared," Jaye said.

"Airin and I have seen magic," Arlene said, "but not here."

"Magic hasn't disappeared. It's gone underground. We have a magic-wielding enemy, and that's a problem for us." Jaye stopped at a traffic light and shivered at the memory of Enauria blasting him with lightning.

"Airin didn't declare the sword to customs."

Jaye narrowed his left eye and looked at Arlene. "It might have magic and could be useful. Consider getting him released. If he's deported back to Landen, you'll lose your opportunity." He sped when the light turned green. "Tell me about the sword."

"The Atrinisy Blade is poshy and svelte. Airin made it vanish and reappear at will. There's a reason the sword has to be in Aleria, but he didn't say."

"Maybe he's connected to Enauria." Jaye called Kyle, but the voicemail answered. "Kyle, see if you can get Airin released from holding. I know he doesn't have a celestial passport, but we have to keep him close." Jaye hung up the phone.

"Airin's gonna need a cover."

"I'll let Kyle handle that. He's good at filling in backstories."

Twenty minutes passed. In a suburb of West Scarlet devoid of high-rises, Jaye steered the car with one hand and slowed as he approached the Juniper Café, a two-story restaurant with no outdoor seating. Exquisite glass trees bathed the café's terrace in light at nighttime.

Windshield wipers swept droplets away. Jaye parked the car, disengaged the key, and escorted Arlene to the café. Arlene stopped to look at the café, and Jaye admired it with her in the light rain. The Juniper Café had no name on its concrete, steel, and glass exterior. An alabaster, fern, and onyx insignia marked the restaurant for customers. Jaye hoped the food lived up to its reviews. "Arlene, I'm on my last assignment."

"What? Dinner?"

"No, although that wouldn't be a bad choice."

Arlene changed her tone. "Del A Cruise know this?"

"He approved it. Once it's over, I'm out." Jaye wished he had said the words years ago. He tugged Arlene's hand but did not hold it. "Come on, I'm buying."

Arlene started the night with a glass of Vesrynel. The violet-colored liqueur was famous for its tendency to evaporate when exported off Aleria. Jaye opted for something lighter and settled on wine.

Throughout dinner, electronic music with no vocals played. Upbeat songs made Jaye bob his head, and Arlene did the same with mellow and ambient tracks.

"So, where do we stand? With us?" Jaye said. "When we were together, you left me because your father offered me my job."

Arlene chuckled. "I left you because of what you do and because my father gave it to you. He knew how to get you out of my life."

"I never thought of it that way. Why didn't you tell me?"

"Because you needed Infinity to impress my father."

"No, I didn't."

"You needed it for yourself."

Jaye blinked at Arlene's brutal honesty and shifted back in his seat. Her words were not new, but this time, he gave no argument.

"I despise your job because it separated us."

Jaye imagined leaning over the table and taking Arlene's face in his hands, kissing her. "I love you, and I know we can still be happy."

Arlene picked up her glass and held Jaye's hand. "I'll toast to that."

Aperture 20

Airin examined his clean-shaven, partial reflection in the window and adjusted the zipper of his new black-and-charcoal-gray jacket. The jacket smelled store-bought, and he missed having a chained timepiece in a vest pocket. He touched the crisp fabric of the jacket at the wrist and pressed on a metal, but foreign, wristwatch underneath. He was a tourist—worse, a tagalong. Idleness made Airin's freedom bittersweet, and he craved more than retaining the sword on Aleria.

The cover provided an opportunity to portray a character: Airin Asariel. He married into Arlene's family and took their surname, the way it was done back home. The white gold ring on his left hand pressed too hard against the skin, so he loosened it with his thumb. Airin continued to observe his reflection in the mirror and rehearsed his full name in his mind. It took a few tries before the name sounded natural. "Airin Asariel."

"That's soundproof," a technician said. "They can't hear you."

Airin looked past his reflection into an interrogation room with recessed lighting, a desk, two security guards, Garindae, a two-member interrogation team, and Arlene.

"Veylen Garindae," the female interrogator said, "you've served time in prison for drug charges when you were a teenager but have avoided arrest since."

The male interrogator reviewed a folder. "Your file says you were never in the military, never a businessman, or a politician, but you knew the people who took over Nonpareil. Some were your college classmates, and others became your friends. Their business became your way of life."

The female interrogator took over. "Here's what you are: an apprentice to networking, corruption, and survival, inheriting a paramilitary and fleeing Nonpareil after attacking the East Coast of the United States in an act of terrorism."

Behind the glass, two other people watched the interrogation. They had escorted Arlene into the room. She seemed close with the man named Jaye, but didn't interact with his associate in the dark peacoat.

After a few minutes of talking, the interrogators asked what Arlene knew about Garindae. Arlene folded her hands across the table, leaned in, and propped her shoulders forward. "After the Massive Plunge"—Arlene looked to the male interrogator at her right—"Garindae used the instability of the country to lock up the government, turn it on itself and everyone else."

"You helped turn Nonpareil into a stratocracy," the male interrogator said. "Your coconspirators are dead. Killed in the attack, or prior to it."

The female interrogator stood at the corner of the room, taking notes. "Where is your fleet? The one that attacked West Scarlet?"

Garindae refused to answer questions.

Arlene left the interrogation room and entered the observation area. "I want to kill this guy."

"They'll sentence him with the death penalty on Earth," Jaye said.

"They better." Arlene did not face the window.

Airin wondered if Arlene would have been happy if he had killed Garindae in the plane with the Atrinisy Blade.

"Mr. Garindae," the male interrogator at the desk said, "tomorrow you will be extradited back to Earth. You will face felony charges of terrorism against the United States and felony charges of treason, terrorism, and war crimes against the country of Nonpareil."

The American destroyer *Indigo Viper*, carrying a complement of one hundred fifty personnel and Garindae, traveled through deep space at lightspeed. Jaye flew as a fighter escort with Katherine as his wingman and enjoyed working with her because they made a deadly one-two combination.

"You nickname every plane you fly," Jaye said. "What would you call this one?"

Katherine laughed. "You know, sometimes I come up with the names after the mission."

"Come on, Kat, hit me."

"The Joint Strike Fighter, the Shrike." She paused. "What about *Magpie Shrike*?"

"I think it's a winner. You made me crave pie in space."

Lea-Anne worked in her quarters, completing a duty report for Infinity's stay on Aleria. An address by President Del A Cruise, which was a few days old, played in the background: "I'd like to apologize to the American people for being absent since the Nonpareil attacks. Some of you are outraged."

"They are," Lea-Anne said.

"In this time of crisis, I want to reassure you I did not abandon America when she needed me most."

"They hate you because you're single."

"I was in full contact with the vice president, my cabinet, and the Joint Chiefs of Staff."

"Country's not used to a bachelor president." Lea-Anne signed her name at the bottom of the report. "They liked your ex." She filed the· report away. "You should've married her instead of breaking it off."

The *Indigo Viper* shook, and Lea-Anne clung to her desk. The report fell to the floor and the lights went out. Reserve power came online and filled the room with a dim, darkroom red. An officer gave the command for general quarters. Flash grenades exploded, followed by gunfire inside the ship. "They're trying to break out Garindae." Lea-Anne grabbed her gun, pointed it toward the back of her door, and slid her hand to unlock it.

An explosion roused Garindae, and he fell out of bed. The guard assigned to the cell, who kept him under an unnecessary suicide watch, aimed a gun at his face in the auburn light. "Soldiers are boarding this ship with orders to extract you. They'll kill the guard outside and when that door opens, you either leave with me or die here."

"You're a double-agent," Garindae said.

"Our interests are aligned."

"How?"

The guard kept his eyes and gun trained on Garindae. "You're looking for the Crystal and you have a lead."

Gunfire drew closer and Garindae tried not to let it distract him. He had no leads on a crystal, but he withheld that information from the guard.

"We'll free you and provide you with resources," the guard said. "More than what you had, anyway."

Garindae leered at him, and he hated how the guard used the word "had." "What do I get?"

"That's up to my employer."

An exchange of gunfire took place outside the brig. A body collapsed, and the door opened.

Garindae looked at the dead man and open door. "I'll go under one condition: assassinate President Noel Asariel. Call it in to your employer now."

. . .

Jaye opened a channel. "Kat, I've lost the *Indigo Viper*'s signal. Can you reconfirm?"

"No joy."

"We have to find her."

"Tracing the last known flight path." After a beat, Katherine said, "Got it. She's full stop at these coordinates. Forwarding them to you now."

"Full stop?" Jaye looked at his navigation screen.

"Engine trouble?" Katherine said, unsure.

"No, they would've declared it. Prepare to drop out of lightspeed."

"Copy."

Jaye checked his instruments. "In three, two, one."

Jaye cut his faster-than-light engines, and the plane decelerated. He flew using the plane's inertia and threw in a few maneuvering thruster boosts to glide into a U-turn. Firing reverse thrusters at intervals, followed by a primary thruster boost, counterbalanced the *Delcensia* and stopped its momentum. Jaye punched in new coordinates and respooled his engines for lightspeed.

"Prepare to re-rendezvous with the *Viper*," Jaye said. "She's only a minute or two out. Ready on my mark."

"Set."

"Mark."

Lea-Anne picked up a radio from a dead marine. "Enemy soldiers have boarded the ship, and they're jamming communication to the bridge. They've sealed off aft access and their target's unknown." She examined the area. "I've got multiple dead on deck thirteen. Anyone copy?"

Kyle came on. "Their target's Garindae."

"Merkailer? Where are you?"

"In pursuit."

"How many are there?"

"Eight to ten. Heavily armed."

"Do you have support?" Lea-Anne asked.

"Negative. They're on their way to the aft airlock. They must've secured Garindae."

"Don't engage them without backup."

Kyle said, "I can cut them off."

"Do not engage without backup!"

"No one's coming!" Kyle said. "They killed everyone who's tried to stop them."

"You can be next, dammit."

Kyle's tone changed. "Jenna's dead. The explosion killed her, and someone shot Clarence."

Lea-Anne looked at the ceiling and inhaled. Her heart ached from the deaths of her teammates, and she tightened her grip on the radio. "Merkailer, I know what you're thinking, but fall back. That's an order. I need you alive."

The fleet of enemy ships surrounding the *Indigo Viper* opened fire at Jaye and Katherine when they arrived.

"Evasive maneuvers!" Jaye said. "Break, break, break!"

Jaye stayed in formation with Katherine as they moved away from enemy cannon and missile fire.

"I'm locked on," Katherine said.

"Abort. We can't engage without reinforcements." Jaye grimaced and switched to another channel. "Fherazin-1 to West Scarlet Control. I'm declaring an emergency. The *Indigo Viper* has been ambushed."

"Jaye!"

Several ships launched missiles at the *Indigo Viper*, and some broke through the *Viper*'s anti-projectile cannons.

"No!" Jaye could not bear to see his colleagues die. "I'm attacking them."

"Don't do it! Jaye, you read me?"

Jaye accelerated as another wave of missiles fired and gunned down two missiles, but an outbreak of multiple flashes from waking ships blinded him, so he veered away and drifted to a dead stop. The enemy ships disappeared once the light subsided, leaving the escape shuttles of the *Indigo Viper* to float amidst the wreckage of the ship. "Kat, report."

"No contacts. We're clear."

"Jaye," Lea-Anne said over a shuttle transponder, "Kyle and I are safe. We've got survivors we have to account for."

"Good to hear your voice. I'm glad you're okay." Jaye switched channels. "Kat, stay on watch while we coordinate the rescue."

"Copy that."

"Jaye, Clarence and Jenna are dead," Lea-Anne said. "And Garindae's gone."

Jaye disabled the broadcast and slammed his hand in rage against the controls.

A news ticker about Toronto's G9 Summit did not concern Jaye, but President Del A Cruise paid attention behind an espresso-colored desk inside his office aboard Air Force One. The pilot announced forty minutes until landing. Across from the president, Jaye swiveled his chair and fastened and unfastened a platinum clip over his onyx tie. "Ten days have passed since Garindae's escape, and I can't get over attending premature funerals. The last few years, Clarence played the role of a married guy so well, I expected a wife at the service. I miss that about him. I'm thankful to have served with him—Jenna, too. Best sniper I've ever known. It's sad because she wanted the record for most confirmed sniper kills. They'll be tough to replace."

"I was fond of Clarence and Jenna, and I think about the other men and women who died on board *Indigo Viper*. I don't want those service members to have died for nothing." The president drank coffee from a paper cup. "Earlier, you proposed a theory, and that's what hurts and scares me the most. The theory changes the way we proceed." The coffee cup went back onto a coaster on the desk. "Before I go on, what're your goals in life now?"

Jaye crossed his leg and rested his hands on his right knee. "I want to fly away with Arlene. I miss shredding with my guitar, and I think it'll be fun to record music. Maybe I can persuade Arlene to sing on a few tracks. Do nothing . . . be happy."

"I didn't know she sings."

"She has a great voice when she's drunk."

"That's your dream?"

Jaye nodded. "The start of it."

The president smiled. "Family?"

"Family, dog, house, a place where we can have a good view of the sky." Jaye snapped his fingers. "Some people are about the ocean, but I like the sky. I wouldn't mind having both."

"Hang on to that." The president reached around an elegant wooden chessboard on his desk and slid a deck of cards toward him. "Your theory's right. Covert agents have breached us. Hunting them down will take time, so we leave them in play." He took the cards out of the box, performed a Hindu shuffle, and cut the deck. "This might be sudden, but it's necessary. I'm pulling you from Fherazin Division."

"Short-lived tenure."

"You'll operate unaffiliated and be issued the rank of captain. I'm also pulling Lea-Anne Claire and Katherine Cablarenn."

"Sir?"

"Claire will be issued the rank of major," the president said. "Cablarenn, lieutenant, and Kyle Merkailer, commander. You'll have tactical command that will supersede Claire's rank, and she'll handle your intelligence when you don't require her in the field." He riffle-shuffled the cards in his hands while holding them in the air. "I want you to apprehend Garindae and find out what ties he has with the Syndicate. Report everything to me."

"Yes, sir." Jaye asked, "Planning to show me a trick?"

"No, but you will." The president returned the deck to its box, stood, and gave Jaye the cards. "You're loaded with aces." Jaye pocketed the cards without looking at them. "Good hunting, Captain DiVista."

The interior of Saint Rhiannon Church had tan wood, opal marble, and mirror strips. Black provided a subtle accent near the ceilings and trim of the walls. Over the altar was a large cross assembled from narrow mirrored bars. Crosses reminded Jaye of his father, who had sacrificed his life to save people in an accident.

A priest with a receding hairline entered, and Jaye trailed him through the church until they reached a chamber with three religious statues placed across a table. Natural light filled the room through a stained glass window. Jaye unhooked a broken key from his keychain and showed it to the priest, who reached into his pocket and produced a small case. The priest opened the case and unwrapped a midnight cloth to reveal a pristine key. Jaye exchanged his key for the unbroken one, turned his back, and the priest closed the door.

Minutes later, the door to a private basement opened, uncovering a ladder-like staircase to the Rhiannon Room—a space no larger than the inside of a phone booth. Jaye went down the steps into the dim room, inserted the key into a warded lock on the wall, turned the key, and pulled. A safety-deposit box no longer than a man's wallet came out. Jaye flipped a cover, removed the diamond ring inside, and returned the box to its place. The ring had been concealed for so long, Jaye had forgotten what it looked like. He went upstairs, retraced his way to the body of the church, and walked toward the exit.

Twin hourglasses positioned by the holy water receptacles next to the door worked one minute and stopped. Jaye blinked a few times. The hourglass sands suspended in midair, and Jaye wondered if his eyes were playing tricks on him.

Church doors opened and light flared into Jaye's eyes. He squinted and Enauria entered the parish, wearing a black jacket, a pigeon-colored scarf, and something over her shoulder. Jaye drew his gun and fired. The bullet echoed throughout the church but did not hit. When Jaye squeezed the trigger again, his hand was empty; the gun had vanished. Vertigo kicked in, and Jaye's back slammed against a wall. In the time he took to blink, his location switched from the body of the church to the Rhiannon Room.

Enauria pressed against him and pointed a sword at his neck. The sword lit the room with an evanescent sapphire light, and Jaye cringed because the light had the effect of dry ice. He tried to wrestle the sword from Enauria, but she forced the tip of the blade above his Adam's apple. The ice effect numbed Jaye's chin and throat, and the tip of the blade pricked his skin. Any sudden moves could lead to a punctured throat or decapitation. Jaye scowled. He was so close, he could see her eyes were emerald colored. He turned his head to separate the sword from his neck.

"You can't kill me with a gun," Enauria said. "Now let's try that again."

The freezing cold receded. Enauria's sword dissolved into a wave of temporal light that had the characteristics of water, splitting into waves that flooded up the walls, crept upward over the ceiling, and crashed down onto them. Jaye guessed the water would drown him—except—Enauria opened the church doors, and the twin hourglasses poured sands. Curiosity overtook Jaye, and he walked outside to meet Enauria in front of Saint Rhiannon's mirrored facade.

"Why does a man hide a ring inside a safety-deposit box, locked away in a church?"

Jaye reached into his pocket and touched the engagement ring. "Why do you keep running into me? What do you want?"

"I want to understand how you feel about Arlene, because I'll give you an eternity with her."

Jaye snorted. "If I don't tell you, are we going to do this again and again until I break?"

"Maybe," Enauria said. "Why'd you hide it, Captain DiVista?"

There was no surprise she knew his rank. He wanted to stand his ground and withhold information, but the possibility of being stuck in a time loop was frightening. "I wanted to remind God I love Arlene. I had money, and I used it to fund this church. Donated the rest."

Enauria adjusted the scarf around her neck. "You'll propose to her, but I want you to listen. This is not the way your life is supposed to be."

Jaye turned his back on their reflections. "You don't know my future."

"I know which religions are false. Believe me, I'm experienced with your future." Enauria stepped in front of Jaye, waved her hand, and his gun reappeared. The chamber and magazine were empty. "Protect Airin when the time comes. Don't propose to Arlene. If you propose, somewhere, I'll intervene."

"Define art," Jaye said.

"Alcohol, cigarettes, and your two cents," Arlene said.

"That's a great line."

"Hell yeah, it is."

Jaye held Arlene's glass. "More?"

"Pour. Pour me another." Arlene reached for an empty bottle, but Jaye showed the decanter, and she laughed.

"This is art." Jaye poured red wine into the glass.

"Pouring wine?" Arlene sniffed the bouquet.

"Experiencing what it does." Jaye cozied back up to her.

Arlene lifted the decanter from Jaye's grasp, took his glass and refilled it. With pleasure, she raised her left hand, showing the engagement ring. "This is art. It's goddessy."

Jaye kissed Arlene's hand. She delved into her purse and extracted a cigarette, which he ignited with a cheddar-colored drugstore lighter. He waved the lighter in windshield wiper motions. Arlene smoked and wrapped her arms around his neck with the cigarette still in hand, and kissed him with passion. The decanter knocked over as they tumbled to the floor. Wine soaked their clothes and skin. Jaye caressed Arlene's face, and she extinguished the cigarette with her fingertips. They undressed each other and made love.

The softness of Arlene's skin and sensation of warmth brought pleasure, but Jaye trembled from a battle with his own conscience. He did not deserve Arlene after what he had done six years ago. But guilt and memories would not interrupt his engagement celebration.

. . .

Arlene reveled in ecstasy, closed her eyes, and imagined Jaye was Marshall. With the face of a deceased man in her mind, her eyelids swept up. She made strong eye contact without blinking. "I love you."

Aperture 25

Toronto bustled during the night with traffic and people. Arlene's wet hair numbed the sides of her face and the back of her neck as she stood on the terrace of her hotel suite. She wrapped her arms around her torso, holding a cigarette between her fingers and quivering in the cold. After taking another drag, she dabbed the cigarette against an ashtray to snuff it and flicked the waning butt to the floor. "He's dead."

She poured vodka and looked at her distorted reflection in the glass. The news Jaye had broken earlier in the day consumed her. A headline appeared on the main screen of her phone: "Former U.S. President Asariel Assassinated. Yacht Torpedoed."

Behind her, Airin opened the sliding door, zipped his jacket, and put on gloves.

Arlene slipped the phone into a pocket, stood, tightened the belt on her bathrobe, and carried the drink from the table.

"Jaye and Kyle are still in the meeting," Airin said.

Arlene cried. "It wasn't supposed to be like this."

"I'm sorry about your father." Airin put his hands inside his jacket pockets and continued to stand in the doorway of the terrace, bordering the sanctuary of the bright, heated hotel suite. Arlene's breath evaporated into the nighttime air, and she gripped her drink with such force, the rim of the glass cracked and cut her. Smudgy fingerprints entwined with ash and Arlene imagined her fingerprints had lost her identity. Blood dripped from her hand as she launched the glass into the illuminated metropolis, screaming.

Blueberry and arctic colors lined the dinner coach. Every table had a window and seating for four people, but attendance was sparse. No one sat stag. Kyle walked past a waiter in the aisle who was taking an order and went to the first-class cabins, where bright daffodil lights whisked by from a train on the opposite track. He arrived at a lavender-green door with a small vintage iron plate, mounted at eye level, engraved with a number. Two knocks and nobody answered. Kyle checked to see if anyone was watching, then took out lock picks to work on opening the door. Someone approached, and he stashed the tools in his pocket.

A woman asked in French if Kyle was locked out. With his best poker face, he replied in French that he was. The woman advised Kyle to wait for help, and she went back through the dinner coach. His white lie bought him a few minutes. Kyle pulled out his tools again and picked the lock. When he opened the door, the cabin was empty, so he shut it and retraced his way to the dinner coach.

"I'd like you to have a drink with me."

Kyle stopped to look at the woman who invited him. She was alone—and not his contact. He walked to an empty booth a few seats ahead and sat in the opposite row, diagonal from her. "Thanks, but I'd rather you have the drink with me."

The woman cradled a mixed drink and joined him.

"Who are you?"

"Fiona."

"Fiona . . ." Kyle expected the last name.

"Just Fiona."

"*Just* Fiona?"

"My friends call me Fio, but we're not friends."

Kyle smirked. He liked her style and how her brunette up-do looked warm in the light. Fiona used golden wire hairpins to hold her hair in place. Tiny scepters fastened into the wires and each scepter contained a diamond, complementing Fiona's eyes. "You have the clearest eyes I've ever seen."

"Thank you."

"Sir?" a female porter asked. "Do you still want help with the door?"

Kyle gestured at Fiona. "I'm being taken care of." He waited for privacy as the employee went away. "What're you drinking?"

Fiona answered in Ancient Alerian.

"That's impressive—the drink and the language. I haven't heard it since I moved to Earth," Kyle said.

"What will you be drinking?" Fiona asked, still in tongue.

"An espresso."

"Coffee." She grinned.

"What's wrong with that?"

"Nothing." She gave a mild shake of her head. "I prefer it in the morning."

"It keeps me sharp."

Fiona signaled for a waiter and one responded with a single wave. The waiter looked at her, but she deferred to Kyle, who ordered a triple shot of espresso. The waiter left to get it.

"I want you to meet a friend of mine."

Kyle snickered. "You don't even know my name."

Fiona sipped her drink. "Kyle Merkailer."

She intercepted my liaison, Kyle thought. *That's why no one was in the room.*

Underneath the table, Kyle drew a gun with his left hand so the weapon could not be seen from the passing aisle. He trained the gun so one shot would kill her if she tried to play him, but he hated to waste such a fine woman. "You're well informed. Is that how you found me? Your friend?"

"It is."

"Who's your friend?"

"Her name's Enauria."

The waiter returned with the espresso and set it on the table.

Fiona thanked the waiter in French.

Kyle kept his eyes on Fiona and waited for the server to leave before speaking. "You want me to meet her. What else?"

Fiona finished her drink and waggled the ice in the glass. "Jaye DiVista. Did you know he killed Arlene's ex-fiancé?"

Before meeting Kyle in France, Jaye, Arlene, and Airin made a stop at the Sofia museum in Madrid, Spain. The three studied Pablo Picasso's black-and-white painting *Guernica*. In the artwork, a bull, a horse, people, faces, and severed limbs clustered together.

Jaye concentrated on a man at the far right of the image with his hands up, screaming while trapped in a burning building. He must've looked like this in the Trifecta Towers.

Arlene liked the light bulb drawn inside an eye at the top of the painting, shining a ray of light like the sun, or a fire causing the chaos. The person trampled by a stampede of characters at the bottom left changed her mind and became the best part of the work. If she could change anything in the work, she would make that guy rise and stop the horde.

Airin admired the outstretched arm above the center of the artwork, its hand holding a candle, guiding the stampede with light, away from a door and burning building.

I need direction, Airin thought. *Where are you, Enauria?*

Arlene took Jaye's hand. "This is one of my favorites. Thank you for taking me here."

"One day, I'd like to go back to the MCA in Chicago and stand where we first met."

"Everything's changed."

Jaye wrapped an arm around Arlene and kissed her forehead. "We'll find Garindae and those responsible for the death of your father."

Aperture 28

Brochures told Garindae he was in the Roxy Crimson, a hotel on the planet Novardi, several days away from Aleria. He sat on a lemon-colored sofa, disliked being alone in the room, and hated not being in control. A circular table with a chandelier overhead highlighted a centerpiece of flowers into overexposure. Pink petals seemed orange, and the light spilled over the edge of the table. Garindae hated waiting for hours but understood his new allies needed secrecy and time to talk things over.

A tall brown door with a sand-colored ornamental border opened. Garindae was summoned. He passed through the door, up a cerulean staircase, and into a flame-toned room where a controlled burn had scorched the walls. The charred remains combined with crimson paint, dead trees, and an abundance of chandeliers, varying in brightness.

Two women shot pool near an elaborate bar, and a giant window showed the sun setting over the horizon.

"Would you like a drink?" the blonde asked.

"Vesrynel, if you have it," Garindae said.

"Fine choice."

"I can't get it on Earth."

The bartender, a man with eyeglasses, poured the violet-colored alcohol.

Garindae took the drink from the countertop and walked closer to the pool table. The brunette was an inch taller than her companion, but aside from height, they looked similar, almost like sisters with different-colored hair.

"Do you shoot?" the blonde asked.

Garindae shrugged. "A little."

"Would you like a match?"

"I want to know what's going on."

"Get a cue." The blonde pointed at a triple-columned cue rack built into the wall opposite the bar. The rack had doors of glare-free glass.

"I'm not doing anything until—"

"Garindae, relax." The brunette left the pool game, and the blonde collected the solids and stripes to rack.

Garindae turned and the blonde whispered something into the bartender's ear.

"I can't tell you who I am, but I'll lie to you if that makes you comfortable. You can call me Elle, but what's important is my title," the blonde said. With a loud crack, balls scattered across the billiard felt. "I'm the Trustee."

Garindae selected the heaviest cue. "You agreed to my condition."

"I had nothing to do with assassinating President Asariel," the blonde said.

"Who did?"

"The former Trustee, but he died from cardiac arrest . . . so, you'll deal with me." The blonde cleared shot after shot. "I enjoy pool because it evokes swordsmanship without swords. There's spectacle without anyone getting killed. We both want the Crystal, that's why you're here."

Enauria missed a shot on purpose to give Garindae a turn.

"How do you know about it?" Garindae asked.

"I have visions that guided me to you. That's why I'm in charge."

"I have visions, too."

"Don't you see?" The blonde squared her hands against the edge of the table. "We need each other to find it."

Garindae sighed. "I'm chasing a crystal because a vision tells me to. I don't even want it."

"No?"

"No."

"Not even curious what you could do with it? What could be achieved?"

Garindae stared at the table.

"You'll know the reason," the blonde said, "after you find it."

"So, Elle, what do you propose?"

"You'll have the resources of the Syndicate at your disposal. Your own personal army to find the Crystal."

"The catch?"

"It's divided into two pieces and well hidden," the blonde said. "I'll tell you where to go."

Garindae chalked his cue. "If you know where the pieces are, why don't you get it yourself?"

"Because I'm not supposed to. I can't."

Garindae snorted. "What happens once I get this Crystal? It's supposed to control time. Are we supposed to share it? I don't trust you, and I don't think you'd trust me." He finished his drink. Fired a bank shot. Missed. "We'd betray each other a million times over."

"Once you get the Crystal, you're going to use it to kill me," the blonde said.

The brunette said, "Then you can do whatever you want."

Aperture 29

Someone's hand touched Garindae's arm and he shot awake, hitting an empty bottle of Vesrynel with a forearm. The man caught the bottle and set it on the bar. Garindae rubbed his eyes and stood. Aside from the human alarm clock, the billiard room was empty. The pool table was cleared and the cue cabinet locked. Warm, daytime light filled the room, and the area kept its psychedelic-modern-gothic feel. The light sharpened the imperfections of the burnt wall and the paint streaking across it and cast shadows from dead tree branches.

"Where's the Trustee and the other woman?" Garindae asked.

"We're not allowed to see the Trustee, sir."

"Why are you calling me, 'sir'?"

"Because she transferred us to you," the man said.

"Us? There's only you."

"Members of the organization," he clarified.

Garindae wandered around with slow, restricted movements.

The man said, "I'm supposed to prep you and take you to your ship. Your Nonpareil cruisers have joined, and the fleet is standing by."

"Already?" Garindae grasped his head. "She's a woman of her word."

At a safe house in France that was secured by Kyle, Jaye removed empty water glasses and wineglasses scattered on the dinner table. Arlene sat catatonic in the living room, watching a live broadcast interfaced with French subtitles. A plate of angel hair pasta with beef and Alfredo sauce, cooked two hours earlier, was cold on the coffee table in front of her. A quarter of the plate had been eaten, but the garlic bread Kyle had brought wasn't touched. Twenty minutes had passed since she last moved.

Arlene's oversized sunglasses hid her face, and she had a new, messy hairstyle with black, blond, and auburn streaks. Pink highlights ran down the longer strands. The look revitalized her at the expense of appearing mishmash.

Next to the sofa were three large shopping bags emblazoned with the brand name Divine Discontent, written in French.

Jaye clasped his hands behind his back and thought, *She hasn't even finished one glass of wine.*

Kyle watched the broadcast from behind the kitchen counter while making tea. Airin washed the dishes and put them away. Once he finished, he sat on a chair near Arlene, without disrupting her. Jaye wanted to sit by her and offer words of comfort, but she would shut him out, so he avoided the rejection.

"I can't even attend my father's funeral," Arlene said. "I have to fucking watch it on TV."

A somber melody was performed on a pipe organ, and the camera showed different angles of Saint Matthew's Romanesque interior. Jaye sniffled but held back his tears. Arlene deserved to attend the funeral, even with the estrangement, but her stubbornness prevented a reunion. Jaye prayed for the soul of President Asariel and wished they could have seen the burial.

Later that night, Jaye sat alone on the couch.

Kyle approached. "Where's Arlene?"

"Asleep. She finished the funeral and went straight to bed."

"What about Airin?"

"He's in his room. Why?"

Kyle said, "Garindae is going to Sel Tresel, Monterno. We can intercept him in eight days."

"I'm glad you got new intel. What's your source?"

"Jaye, how many times have you met Enauria?"

"Twice."

"You don't talk about her."

"It's in the report."

"Has she mentioned anyone else?"

Jaye shook his head.

"Enauria has a friend," Kyle said.

"Is that your source? Enauria's friend tell you something about the future? Something useful?"

"I know there's a lot going on, but you should watch your tone. Enauria's friend is Princess Fiona Straeis-Ascaria."

"Remind me."

"The daughter of Queen Caneria," Kyle said. "In Enauria's dossier, Caneria was Enauria's close friend who disappeared in the middle of her reign. Fiona was supposed to inherit the crown, but she abdicated, and if you go back to Aleria, they'll tell you she's been missing, too, a couple hundred years."

Jaye stood and moved to the kitchen.

"I met Fiona on a train," Kyle said. "On the way to Paris. Enauria too. They took me to a hotel and disguised me as a bartender—"

"What?"

"I saw Garindae and Enauria talking while shooting pool. Enauria's the source, if you want to know. But that's not what I want to talk to you about."

"Then what is?"

"Before we ship out . . ." Kyle looked upstairs and moved, signaling Jaye to follow him into a hallway deprived of light. Kyle lowered his voice to a whisper. "Is it true you killed Arlene's ex-fiancé?"

No one had asked Jaye to tell the truth about Arlene's ex-fiancé in a long time. President Asariel had issued an order, and he had followed through. Before the mission, the president never said

Arlene's fiancé traveled onboard a hijacked plane. If only he knew the fiancé was there, he wouldn't have destroyed the plane. He could never confess. If Arlene ever found out he shot a missile that had killed the one she loved, she would hate him more for having joined Infinity, and their relationship would be ruined. Jaye lied to Kyle without the slightest hesitation.

Monterno was a rare planet where a beautiful view of the sky could cause a seizure for the wrong person. The planet's axis and orbit around its sun caused a constant state of time-lapse photography in the sky. Lamplights turned off, and sunlight brightened a crowded bridge and its surroundings. A day had finished in minutes. Jaye waited for the next change in the unpredictable night-and-day cycle. The sun and clouds moved at a blistering pace. Lamplights grew warmer in radiance as daylight shifted into night. Schizophrenic sunsets were Jaye's favorite.

People crossed back and forth along the steel suspension footbridge. Most of the locals were between the ages of thirty and fifty. They exuded a catwalk attitude to distinguish themselves from tourists who stopped to admire the sky or antique iron lampposts lining the bridge with a rusty, yellowish glow when the sky was dark. Waterfalls plunged above the bridge, producing mist that would have formed a rainbow on Earth. Three of Monterno's four moons were visible, but they were golden instead of white.

The wind picked up strength and sent a cold gust against Jaye's face. He imagined strolling with Arlene around the city, taking pictures of each other and together. He regretted her absence. Halfway across the bridge, Jaye stopped. Flocks of people went around him. The careless ones bumped into his shoulders, but he kept his eyes on Garindae, who faced the rails. Garindae needed to be captured alive.

Sel Tresel was a city designed with verticality. Buildings were arranged in tiers, surrounded by verdant hills, sanded cliffs, low-pressure waterfalls, and fog. The structures were a mix of old stone buildings and modern skyscrapers. Lea-Anne had grown tired of many cities looking the same, so she appreciated how Sel Tresel distinguished itself by being a foot-traffic city. Highways and automobile roads existed outside of downtown.

From the window of a building, Lea-Anne observed Garindae through the scope on a sniper rifle and targeted his legs. The shot was easy. If Garindae fled, he would not go farther than a yard.

Arlene peered through binoculars from another building's window, scouting the bridge and struggling to find Garindae through the mass of people crossing. "These tourists are screwing with my shot."

She held the binocs with her right hand, traced her fingers down the left side of her neck, and flicked her hair. Locals moved. Tourists took pictures and enjoyed the sights. Garindae was alone and without a camera. Easy prey.

"I found you." Arlene zoomed in on his face to confirm her target.

Hash marks from an enemy sniper focused on Jaye.

Lying prone, Arlene set the binoculars down and looked through the scope of a sniper rifle she had rigged on top of a table. The crosshairs lingered on Garindae's head but swayed. Arlene had never fired a weapon intending to kill. She placed her finger over the trigger and took a deep breath.

Colors alternated between night and day. Each of the snipers had to switch from normal to night vision to compensate for the bizarre change of atmosphere. Firing any shot would be a challenge because none of the snipers knew how long their shooting conditions would last. At one moment they would see through a dark-greenish lens, turning off night vision as dawn emerged.

Jaye lurked in the throng of people, drew his weapon, and closed in on Garindae, intending to use a takedown. A suppressed bullet shredded through the wind, sailed past Garindae, and hit the floor. Garindae ducked and fled for cover.

Jaye yelled Garindae's name.

More sniper bullets. More misses.

The crowd dispersed. A civilian next to Jaye was shot and fell dead.

"I'm taking fire." Jaye ran after Garindae and thought the sniper targeting Garindae was sloppy because the shooter failed to compensate for wind speed.

Airin was not on the bridge, but as gunfire erupted, he rushed over it, shouting for Jaye to get down, and then pounced on him the way a bodyguard would. Airin took a bullet in the back. Body armor absorbed the shot, but the impact made him drop his gun.

At the mouth of the bridge, Kyle pointed an assault rifle toward a window and unleashed a burst to distract the sniper, and he provided a stream of cover fire in intervals.

Lea-Anne sent an armor-piercing bullet through a window, ending the enemy sharpshooter's life, but perceived more shooters were at large.

Jaye checked on Airin. There was no bleeding, so he took off after Garindae, yelling Garindae's name so loud it strained his throat. The crowd of civilians and the light shifting into darkness masked Garindae, but Jaye pursued.

Arlene trained her night vision scope on Garindae and fired, but stress and the winds of Sel Tresel made her shots go astray. The magazine depleted faster than expected. Garindae would be gone if she had to reload, so she stopped firing and waited for the best shot.

"There's a sniper on Garindae," Lea-Anne said.

"We need Garindae alive. Take the sniper out," Jaye said.

"Copy that," Lea-Anne said. "Merkailer?"

"It's coming from the tower next to you," Kyle said. "You have no shot."

Lea-Anne deferred. "Katherine."

"I'm on it." Katherine repositioned her scope and tracked with thermal scanning. She blew a bubble with her chewing gum.

Kyle ran across the bridge, hoping no one would shoot him. He checked Airin, helped him up, and escorted him to safety. Snipers fired at each other, and Kyle had too much adrenaline to flinch. He considered himself lucky to be alive.

Daylight took over and Lea-Anne pinpointed another shooter. As a rule, she hated Monterno's environmental changes, but she loved them when they worked in her favor. Another casing from her rifle fell onto the floor.

The wind died. Arlene followed Jaye as he sprinted after Garindae. She reset her grip on the rifle, took a diver's breath, and depressed the trigger.

Katherine fired a shot at Arlene without knowing it was her.

Enauria generated a blaze of teleporting light to sway the outcome. Darkness came again.

The sounds of police and emergency medical vehicles filled the air, along with the sight of flashing sirens in the kaleidoscopic night.

Aperture 31

Lea-Anne made a call inside a dim hotel room. "Mister President, Veylen Garindae is dead." She listened to the president. "No, sir. We don't have his body. Forensics might have recovered it. Lieutenant Cablarenn is trying to confirm." She waited for her turn to speak. "Some kind of EMP went off. Captain DiVista, Commander Merkailer, and Airin Asariel have disappeared." She winced and looked at bright floral patterns on the bed. "Arlene Asariel is also missing." She bit her lip. "She wasn't included in the op because Jaye said she shouldn't be there."

The president took a moment and said, "I'm reinstating Infinity."

In a half-somber, half-cheerful tone, Lea-Anne said, "Thank you, sir."

"Cablarenn will be your XO. Reassemble the team. Find Jaye and his crew. Whatever it takes."

From the penthouse, Kyle recognized the shrine of Fherazin Venar and its gold-accented rotunda a few blocks away. He was in the Shrine City of Fherazin, a couple hundred kilometers from West Scarlet. The city was at a standstill. Power was off, and candlelight was the only light source scattered throughout downtown—except for the shrine of Fherazin herself, and the skyscraper he was in.

"Enauria teleported me again and stripped my gear. How irritating." Kyle stood on a granite-trimmed balcony overlooking an in-house swimming pool, which flowed to an infinity pool on the outdoor balcony. Golden lights brightened the indoor pool; azure bulbs lined the exterior pool. "This is fancy. It'd be nice to take a swim."

At the balcony's right wing, a pair of oval tables held abstract art—statues of items and animals, both real and fantastic. One statue had a person standing next to a geared clock showing fifteen hours in a day. Kyle raised his sleeve from the wrist and watched the hands on his chronometer spin in disarray. "What the hell?"

Kyle heard two familiar female voices talking downstairs, so he descended a spiral staircase of glass steps. Frosted patterns like kindergarten doodles were etched into each step. Kyle went down the stairs cautiously, hugging the banister to ensure silence, and peeked over a maroon wall at the bottom of the stairs.

Behind a lavastone counter, Enauria held a glass that was two sips away from empty. Fiona was opposite Enauria, occupying a slender barstool with legs crossed. She poured Vesrynel into an empty glass and placed it at the counter's end.

"Why don't you join us?" said Enauria.

Kyle approached. "What now? I'm tired of surprises."

Enauria came around the counter, took the drink Fiona had

poured and offered it. Kyle cradled the drink with a lack of interest.

"To my cousin Fherazin." Enauria toasted Kyle's glass.

The clang made Enauria grin, but Kyle listened to it in contempt while Enauria finished the Vesrynel. "I don't care for your cousin."

Fiona stood in a hurry, stamping her foot, and holding a combative posture. The way she glared made Kyle realize he could not take back what he had said. Enauria delivered a heavy shove, tripping him. Kyle winced at her power and quickness as he hit the floor with a thud. Enauria snatched his wrist, dragged him grunting, writing, and shouting across the penthouse. She hurled him into the heated swimming pool. The impact from being launched charged Kyle with more adrenaline, and he fought his way to the water's surface, raced to the pool's edge, and grabbed Enauria's left ankle, but she backed away from his reach.

Kyle imagined wrenching Enauria into the water. He pictured them grappling and water splashing as he tried to secure her. When she maneuvered away from his grasp, he pulled her hair hard, yanking her head and causing a squeal. He made a fist and pummeled her face. Blood formed around Enauria's lip and streamed out her nose, contaminating the water.

Fiona walked to the pool before Kyle could climb out. "It's Fherazin's death anniversary today, but you don't care for a woman who helped save this world. You don't have respect." She stretched her arm, aimed an index finger at Kyle, and drew swirls in the air. The water spun underneath Kyle and constricted him, elevating his body into the air where he hung, suspended. Fiona dug her index finger into her palm and Kyle screamed when the water conducted electricity.

"I didn't know it was today," Kyle said. "I'm sorry!"

On the verge of passing out, Kyle sighed as the spell ended and the pain subsided. Several armed officers of the Royal Guard came through the penthouse doors and secured positions around the room.

Enauria tied back her hair and watched Fiona, who looked at the cyclone of silent current that held Kyle.

Facing the guard captain, Fiona said in Ancient Alerian, "Please leave. We must talk to this man alone."

Kyle lay on his left side, shirtless, facing the window and shivering. He grinned because his body did not have burns from the lightning. There was no soreness. Not even the faintest trace of a headache. The floor tiles were blurry, so he rubbed his eyes and waited for his eyesight to clear. When the tiles sharpened into focus, Kyle was relieved his vision had not been damaged. He rolled onto his stomach and pushed up from the cold floor. To keep warm, he crossed his arms over his chest. Beyond the penthouse windows, the crisp, yellow jacket colors of the Shrine City did not inspire him. Home seemed far away. Kyle wanted to be anywhere other than the Shrine City, and he longed to be in the company of those he knew and trusted. Enauria was in the kitchen, but he chose not to make eye contact. Facing the consequences of upsetting her or Fiona was not something he wanted to do.

A new shirt and jacket were draped over a barstool. Kyle inspected the clothes and checked the tags for sizes. The shirt was fine, but the jacket was loose. Dry clothes were better than no clothes, so he put them on and tugged the back of the jacket to make it snug on his body. His pants were still wet and his shoes were floating in the pool. Shoes weren't important at the moment, so he took his socks off and walked barefoot.

In the kitchen, Enauria ate from an assortment of sliced fruit arranged in a white serving bowl. Her flawless face and casual attitude showed no grudge for what he had said earlier. Kyle clenched his hand and seethed. He wanted information from Enauria before he could let go of their clash.

Enauria held Kyle's watch in her hand. "Catch," she said, tossing the timepiece.

Kyle caught the watch with one hand and fastened it to his wrist. The hands continued to spin. "Why's it like this?"

"Because you're in the future."

"This is the future?" Kyle looked outside. The future did not look different. "What am I doing here?"

"I brought you here because I can't work in the past. Not the way I used to."

Kyle tried to make sense of what she had said.

Enauria pointed her finger at the lavastone counter and tapped it. "This is the present, for me." She pointed her finger at him. "It's a hundred years later for you." Enauria reached for another bottle of Vesrynel, took her glass, refilled it, and fixed her eyes on Kyle again. "Care for some?"

"I'll pass," Kyle said. "Don't you drink anything else?"

"I do, but if you don't want to drink, that's your loss."

Kyle took a seat at the stool Fiona had used earlier. Enauria sipped her Vesrynel, and Kyle looked at the fruit bowl. More than a quarter of the fruit was gone.

"Imagine you have a job," Enauria said. "Jobs have obstacles. Do you let obstacles get in the way of finishing your work?"

"No."

Enauria took a fork near the side of the bowl and picked a slice of fruit, which she emphasized to Kyle. "This is what I have to get to." She placed the fruit into the empty quarter of the bowl and traced the fork in a circle around the vacant space. "This is a firewall."

Kyle stared at the glossy white space, imagining a field of energy.

"Let's say Jaye does something. Here's the result." Enauria nudged the isolated fruit. "Then Airin." She extended her arm high to suspend the bowl high in the air. "Then Arlene." She waved the fork in a half-crescent motion and separated the underside of the bowl containing the fruit slice. The bowl fragment and fruit fell onto the counter.

Kyle imagined Enauria performing street magic and succeeding as an illusionist.

"That's what your colleagues are doing," Enauria said. "Moving things into position." She set the bowl aside and stabbed the fruit with the tip of the fork. "So I can do my job."

The fork hit the counter. Kyle straightened and gripped the counter's beveled edge. "What's the job? Getting the Crystal so that you can kill yourself?"

Enauria scoffed and concealed a smirk by a marginal turn of her head and a slight shake of her blond hair.

"No metaphors," Kyle said. "Tell it straight."

Enauria walked around the counter and whispered into Kyle's ear, "I'm trying to kill a spirit."

Kyle studied the fruit impaled on the fork and thought, *She's out of her mind.*

Aperture 34

Jaye woke in a chamber painted white, with an aquamarine trim. Light came through the walls, not from fixtures. The ceiling was low, and the ground sloped upward, showing an uneven concrete surface. A ladder mounted onto a wall behind Jaye had rust-free steps, discolored with age. There was a hatch above the ladder— the kind inside a military vessel or underground bunker. The hatch reminded Jaye of a game where one had to point out the out-of-place object in a photo. Jaye grabbed the ladder and tested its sturdiness, climbed a few steps, and stopped at a square plate engraved in archaic symbols. The symbols resembled Egyptian hieroglyphics but were not from Earth. "I'll bet this says keep out." Jaye climbed farther, made a fist, and banged against the hatch. The hatch was as thick as tank armor, and pounding caused an echo. Jaye was in no hurry to discover what was beyond the metal.

Two pairs of footsteps approached. He balanced one foot on the ladder and turned sideways to face Airin and Arlene. "Glad you're here."

"We were on the other side of the hall," Airin said.

"Airin," Jaye said, "are you injured?"

"Just a bruise. I'll be fine." Airin reached over his shoulder and massaged where the bullet had hit him earlier.

"Where are we?" Arlene asked. "What happened to Garindae? Is he dead?"

Jaye said, "We weren't supposed to kill him, Arlene. Only bring him in."

"I shot him. I want to know if he's dead."

Jaye slid down the ladder and hopped onto the ground. "You were the sniper? You know you could've killed me on the bridge. The wind was—"

"You're fine."

Airin stepped away from Arlene.

Jaye said, "That's not the point."

She shrugged.

"You're not professional," Jaye said.

"I can handle a—"

"I don't care if you can handle it or not. You weren't supposed to be there."

"But I was."

"Arlene . . ."

"What, Jaye? What?"

"Nothing! It's done." Jaye looked at Airin and changed his tone. "Any idea where we are?"

"I've never seen this place."

"There's this." Jaye pointed to the hatch. "Don't know where it leads to, so I'm not opening it. Anything else?"

Airin said, "There's another door on the far end. I'll get a closer look at it."

"Jaye, look at me," Arlene said. "He killed my father."

"You didn't like your father."

"I would have reconciled with him."

"When?"

"When I was ready. Garindae took that away from me."

"You feel better 'bout yourself?" Jaye asked.

Arlene opened her mouth to say something but sealed her lips and walked away to ally herself with Airin.

Jaye grabbed her wrist. She fended him off, but he cut in front of her. "Do you?"

"I'll feel better when I know he's dead."

"No, you won't."

"They would've done the same thing anyway . . . killed him on Earth."

"We needed him for intel."

"Screw intel," Arlene said. "Garindae would've given us nothing useful."

"So, you brought him to justice?"

"How many people have you killed, Jaye?"

Jaye's arm went numb.

"How many?" Arlene waited. "You feel good serving your country? Assassinating people? You do it *so* well."

Jaye tried to curl the fingers in his right hand. Nothing happened.

"The world's such a better place because of your work."

"Go fuck yourself," Jaye said.

Arlene did not flinch. "I will. It's better than fucking you."

Jaye wanted to lash out, but arguing was pointless. Both of them had to cool off. He stormed away from Arlene, who did not pursue, and walked to Airin at the opposite end of the chamber.

Airin tried to force the locking mechanism of a vault-style metal door surrounded by rock. When Airin could not break the door open, Jaye tightened his grip on the north and south handles, turning clockwise and counterclockwise, but the door remained shut.

Jaye shouted and kicked the wall, shook the handles, and let go. With a sigh, he ran his hands through his hair and dropped them to his thighs.

Airin said, "The lock's strong, or maybe it's sealed from the other side."

"I'm over it." Jaye rubbed his temples. "Thanks for helping me on the bridge."

"It's good to see action again. Just didn't want to get shot." Airin looked in the direction where Arlene was. "Are you two okay?"

"This happens," Jaye said. "We'll be fine."

"I'm frustrated, too. Life's out of my control," Airin said.

"It is."

They laughed.

Airin summoned the Atrinisy Blade. "Arlene and I had to take this to Aleria. We did, and I don't know what else I'm supposed to be doing, aside from following you. My contact abandoned me." Airin struck the metal door with the sword in frustration, and the clash made Jaye's ears tingle.

"What're you supposed to get for taking the sword to Aleria?"

"I used to serve in the military a few years ago. In the middle of battle, I accidentally fired upon the crown prince, who led our unit. I didn't kill him, but I got a court-martial, demotion, prison time, and a discharge. This sword's my ticket to clearing my record."

"I'd love to make the red in my file disappear. If I were you, I'd take that offer too," Jaye said.

Arlene screamed in the distance—a life-or-death kind of scream that canceled the irritation Jaye had for her. The chamber trembled and the door rattled. Pressure had built behind the wall. "Run!" Jaye said.

Water burst through the door in front of them. The frigid water volleyed into the chamber, knocking both men off their feet. Airin lost the sword to the current. Jaye took a heavy breath and reached for the weapon but missed when it sank underwater. He swam through the deafening rapids, bobbing to the surface every few seconds, but the water was relentless and it manifested the fear of drowning. The water rose toward the ceiling, darkening the room and cutting off oxygen. Jaye preferred to die in a face-off or in the *Delcensia*. Slow deaths were unspectacular.

In the dim study of the penthouse, Kyle fixed his hair while looking at his reflection in a wall-mounted mirror. After he finished grooming, his eyes drifted to a sparse bookshelf and noticed several books about painting watercolors. *She paints*, he thought. He wondered if her work was good. He hadn't seen any paintings here.

A floor lamp stood next to the bookshelf. Kyle turned the lamp on, and the low-wattage bulb shed light on a shadowed area and revealed a portfolio of sheet music. He drew the folder from the shelf and combed through its pages. The folder compiled over fifteen songs. Kyle failed to recognize the titles, composers, or notes. Fiona entered the study, and Kyle had no time to shelve the portfolio or hide it, so he lowered the collection to the side of his leg.

"Do you know what those are?" Fiona asked.

"Notes," Kyle said.

"They're records, encrypted as music."

"Records of what?"

"Everyone involved in the conspiracy to assassinate my mother," Fiona said. "A glorious hit list."

"I'm sorry."

"Enauria and I . . . we're both daughters of the crown. The difference is, I get to continue my mother's legacy."

"And Enauria?"

Fiona gestured for Kyle to follow her out of the study, and they walked to the kitchen and living room. Several candles accented the living area, but in contrast, the pool was dark, except for the outside light that came through the glass. Enauria was absent, but Kyle assumed she was upstairs because lamps were on.

"Enauria promised me she'd hunt everyone responsible," Fiona said, flanked by the tables with abstract artwork and candles.

"Did she?"

"She killed them one by one. This was some time ago." Fiona went to the kitchen, poured a drink, and walked back to Kyle, eying the sheet music in his hand. "May I?"

Kyle passed the records to her, and she thumbed through them.

"She told Jaye there was one left but wasn't specific," Kyle said.

"Enauria has watched over me. It's my turn to help her by convincing you."

"To do what?" Kyle drew a glass hanging inside a see-through cabinet and poured from Fiona's Vesrynel bottle, even though he was not in the mood to drink.

"Convince your friends she isn't your enemy."

Kyle went to the window to admire the Shrine City of Fherazin. He sipped, and the citrusy flavor energized his taste buds, so he finished the rest of the glass. Fiona placed the sheet music on one of the barstools.

"I'd like to call you Fio," Kyle said. "Not Your Highness. Not Fiona." He was not flirting, even though he found her attractive. This was business. Fiona grinned, and he moved closer to her but not close enough to violate her space.

"Only if you help her."

Enauria controlled the water to push the Atrinisy Blade to a dividing wall, where the sword collided and stuck. Rings of red light formed around the wall and the chamber separated into different levels. The floor shifted outward and the wall stretched into a vertical pillar with a metal staircase wrapped around it. Each stair glowed red.

Jaye gasped for air as water flushed out through the break points. His face pressed against the cold rock floor and he rubbed water out of his eyes. He wanted to stand, but his body would not cooperate yet. The air chilled his hands and face. Wet clothes clung to his skin. The white light that had filled the room before returned.

Jaye heard footsteps.

"I lost the Atrinisy Blade," Airin said.

Jaye pushed up and stood. "Where's Arlene?"

Airin helped Jaye get his balance. "Don't know, but we should find her and the sword. There's something you should see."

They approached the stairs. A draft of colder air came from upstairs. Jaye rubbed his arms and crossed them over his chest, looking at a mishmash of red-lit steps.

"What do you think?" Airin asked.

Jaye did not want to know what came next. Surprises tired him, but remaining trapped on the first floor left no other option than to continue upward. Jaye drew his gun and thought, *Find Arlene. Apologize. Find a way home.* "I'll take point."

He and Airin climbed the stairs to the summit. Straight ahead, Arlene held the Atrinisy Blade in her right hand. The relief he had seeing her alive disappeared when she raised the sword against Enauria and warned her not to come closer. Both women stood in the middle of a wet hexagon platform: metal lined the outer layers, glass composed the middle, and stone formed the center.

The platform had no ceiling—only a cloudless midnight sky. Moonlight touched the surface of the platform, showing puddles and droplets. Upward-flowing waterfalls formed a circle around the platform, and the moonlight made the water shimmer.

In the center of the platform was an empty pedestal underneath four pillars supporting a pagoda-shaped roof. Vines with spires of copper flowers Jaye had never seen before enlaced the pillars. Broken glass was on the floor near the pedestal. Arlene clutched her left hand, keeping something from Enauria.

Jaye aimed his gun at Enauria and called Arlene's name.

Airin took cover behind Jaye since he was without a weapon. He speculated Enauria had shown Arlene more magic, and Arlene was threatened by it. He wanted to know if Arlene had found the sword or if Enauria had given it to her. Whatever the circumstance, he hoped his contract with Enauria would remain unchanged. The sword was his responsibility, and he had to get it back. He gazed at the Atrinisy Blade and tried to mentally recall it, but nothing happened, so he tried again with intense concentration. The blade stayed with Arlene. After the third try, he realized the ability to summon and disappear the weapon was a privilege given to the person wielding it.

Arlene heard Jaye's voice and thanked God he was alive, but she never broke her focus on Enauria. "Get me, Jaye, and Airin out of here."

"I can't," Enauria said.

"Liar." Arlene turned her hand and gave Enauria a glimpse of the slanted, three-inch-tall blue-and-white Crystal. "Is this what you want?"

"It is."

The Crystal weighed the same as a small metallic lighter; was cool to the touch; and had smooth, flat faces. Only the top edge felt sharp against the skin. Arlene hid the Crystal behind her back. "I'll throw this into the water if you can't take us away from here."

"Don't."

"Give me a reason."

"Because it'll disappear, and we'll never see it again."

Arlene inched her feet to the left while thinking she would make a move for the corner of the platform and pitch the Crystal away. "I don't care."

Jaye said, "Arlene, walk toward me."

"If you throw it away, you'll ruin your life," Enauria said.

"It's already ruined."

Enauria looked at Jaye, then zeroed in on Arlene. "You have someone to live for."

"Arlene!" Jaye said.

Arlene refastened her grip on the Atrinisy Blade.

Enauria followed the sword move. "Do you know how to use that?"

Arlene had no experience using swords but figured a lightweight sword could not differ from trying to stab someone with an oversized knife.

"Arlene!" Jaye said. "Come on!"

"If you want out of here, you must trust me," Enauria said.

"We want out of here."

"The Crystal. Please."

"No. You first."

A flash of light and a gust of cold air and water blew in various directions when a plane waked above Airin and Jaye. Kyle's voice came through a PA system. "Arlene, it's Kyle. I'm lowering the rescue plate. Give her the Crystal and get onboard. Let's go home."

Bomb bay doors opened, revealing a rescue ladder and retrieval plate. A spotlight from the aircraft swiveled, focusing on her and Enauria.

"Tricks," Arlene said.

"It's not a trick," Enauria said.

"Jaye, check it!" Arlene's gaze stayed on Enauria.

"Airin, go." Jaye pointed to the plane.

Airin ran toward the L-shaped ladder.

"Jaye, you too," Kyle said.

"Not without Arlene."

"Enauria isn't our enemy." Kyle adjusted the spotlight. "She's not here to hurt us. Don't delay her. Give her what she wants so we can go."

"You're not going to give it, are you?" Enauria took two steps toward Arlene.

Jaye nodded at Airin while the L-shaped ladder retracted inside the aircraft. He held his gun steady with two hands, and centered the crosshairs. Enauria had made the gun disappear the first time he tried to shoot her. This was a new opportunity to fire and land a shot.

"Arlene," Enauria said, "Jaye killed Marshall."

Jaye uttered a loud cry when Enauria divulged his secret. He opened fire and ran toward Enauria, but she dissolved the bullets in midair. The gun clicked on an empty magazine. Not a single shot had touched her.

"He killed your ex-fiancé," Enauria said.

Arlene staggered and lowered the Crystal by her left thigh.

Kyle's plane moved, and Enauria teleported the aircraft and herself from the field. Scattered trails and ribbons of fading silver light lingered over the platform. Jaye stopped in front of Arlene but kept his distance from the reach of the Atrinisy Blade.

"Is it true?"

"Arlene . . ." Jaye dropped his gun on the platform, knowing there would be no way to redeem himself from the truth.

"Well?"

Jaye looked downward. "I didn't know he was aboard."

Arlene cried, her lips, jaw, and hands trembling. She tightened her grip in rage. The Crystal picked up her energy.

"It was a hijacked passenger jet," Jaye said. "Your father gave the order. I carried it out."

Arlene released the Atrinisy Blade, and it clanged when it struck the ground. She rushed to Jaye and slapped him. "You motherfucker! I hate you!" A white-hot glow formed around the Crystal. She slapped Jaye harder, and he did not fight back. "I fucking hate you!" She pulled the engagement ring off her finger, still holding the Crystal. "And you wanted to marry me."

She screamed and hurled the ring into the waterfalls. The ring plummeted out of sight, and the Crystal exploded—killing Arlene.

Kyle checked the navigational instruments to verify the plane's location, but the scrambled charts yielded no results. He grunted and activated the autopilot to continue hovering over the ocean with vertical thrust.

Strapped into his seat in the cabin, Airin leaned into the aisle and looked through the open cockpit door to see the night sky outside the aircraft's windshield. He wondered what happened to Jaye, Arlene, and the Atrinisy Blade.

A gust of wind in the aisle chilled the back of Airin's neck. Enauria had teleported onto the plane. He unfastened his safety belt, stood, and blocked the path to the cockpit. "What happened out there?"

Her eyes met Airin's. Questions needed answers, but how much did she have to reveal?

Airin heard a safety buckle unfastening and the quick whip of the belt being flung off a body.

Kyle emerged from the cockpit. "Step aside, Airin."

Airin lowered into his seat and raised an eyebrow when Kyle stepped forward, barefoot.

"Where are we, and what the hell happened?" Kyle said.

"Near the Garden of Arievel," Enauria said.

"Where's that?"

"Landen."

Airin craned his neck to look at Kyle. "It's where I'm from." To Enauria, "I've never heard of it."

Kyle said, "Where are Jaye and Arlene?"

Enauria looked at Airin first, then back to Kyle. "Arlene's dead. I'm sorry."

"Did you kill her?" Airin asked.

"What about Jaye?" Kyle said.

"I didn't kill either of them."

Airin did not believe her.

Kyle said, "I was right above them. I could've done something."

"I saved you," Enauria said. "By sending you away."

"From what?" Kyle said.

Airin rose and flexed one of his hands, loosening his fingers and wrist behind the cover of the chair.

"Don't make a move, Airin," Enauria warned.

Airin imagined himself attacking Enauria and the consequences of doing so. She'd use magic to retaliate, rolling the plane, throwing them around like unsecured baggage. He envisioned a blast of energy ripping a hole through the hull, depressurizing the cabin, while Enauria's magic tore the fuselage apart and sent Kyle and him plummeting to their death. He bit his tongue and shook the thoughts out of his head.

Kyle said, "Jaye was firing at you last I checked."

"I didn't kill them," Enauria said.

"Then, what happened?" Airin said.

"The Crystal exploded and killed Arlene."

"Did you know what would happen?" Kyle strode to Enauria. "What about Jaye?"

"Jaye and Arlene are supposed to die."

"Bullshit!" Kyle smacked the headrest of a chair. "We're all supposed to die."

"That's not what I meant."

"Is that how you rationalize their deaths?" Airin said.

"Jaye and Arlene should have died a long time ago. The missile attack at Nonpareil—remember that?" Enauria didn't wait for an answer. "I saved them from that. They were alive because I did my best to let them live."

Kyle did not look at Enauria.

Enauria continued, "I can control time, but I'm not a higher power. I can't stop things from being how they're meant to be. I can only slow the process. Let me reassure you: I saved Jaye, again."

Turbulence rocked the plane and a proximity alert rang. Kyle ran into the cockpit and rushed into the pilot's seat. "We've got company! It could be a problem since we're not armed." He disabled autopilot, took the controls, and steadied the plane. The strength of the wake's turbulence clued Kyle to a large vessel. Without radar working, he scanned for the ship with his eyes, turned three hundred sixty degrees, and stopped when catching the underside of a ship, hovering ahead.

Kyle steered away and Enauria approached and said, "Kyle, it's okay. The *Seralyn Wave* is Fio's."

The mention of Fiona's name made Kyle loosen his grip on the throttle and stick and reactivate autopilot. He stood and faced Enauria. "What's she doing here?"

"I'm going with her as soon as we're done talking."

Airin joined the conversation and stood behind Enauria.

"Do you need to be picked up? I thought you could teleport wherever you wanted."

"I can," Enauria said. "But I enjoy her company and it's nice to be offered a ride."

Kyle tapped his fingers on the top of the pilot's chair. "If Fiona's here for you, then what about me and Airin?"

"I'll show you how to get back home."

"Will we get our weapons back?" Kyle asked.

"You'll get weapons, but not from me." Enauria chuckled.

"What's funny?" Airin asked.

"I've never used a firearm in my entire life."

"You're kidding," Kyle said.

Enauria spoke with a reflective tone: "I've seen the rise and fall of nations, governments, leaders. I've seen art and life created and destroyed. I've seen weapons of all kinds, but the greatest weapon is the mind."

"I disagree," Kyle said.

Enauria's hand gave a slight tremble. "Do you?"

Kyle shrugged his shoulders. "I think it's magic."

"Bullets sever arteries. Heavy artillery destroys buildings. Magic can do the same," Enauria said. "The difference is, the mind wields magic, and it's powered by the body and soul." She peeked over her shoulder. Airin had his arms folded across his chest. "Great magic—magic that can do more than inflicting pain, like putting thoughts into people's minds or controlling them— needs practice, and it doesn't happen without drawbacks." Enauria walked behind the copilot's chair and leaned an elbow against it. "This'll be the last time I teleport you."

Enauria's hand trembled again. Kyle had never seen her reveal any vulnerability, so maybe she spoke the truth.

"Why?" Airin kept his eyes on Enauria.

"My power to travel through time . . . it's weakening," she said. "I have to make sure you're in the right place. Close to home."

Airin interrupted her. "You looked at Kyle when you said that. What about me? This Crystal you want—it killed Arlene. It'll do the same to us. I'm not helping her find anything. I want reassurances."

"I'm with Airin. I'm not getting you a crystal that can kill me. You still haven't told us what happened to Jaye." Kyle groaned. "You may know what's in our future, that's fine. Fiona says you're a good person, and I'm trying to believe that. If you need our help, start trusting us. We shouldn't be pawns in your personal crusade."

"I'm sorry," Enauria said. "I've been using my power for centuries, controlling everything. I've forgotten how to deal with people." Kyle touched her shoulder, and she looked at him with sincerity. "Thank you for reminding me."

"So . . ." Airin said, breaking the introspective tone.

Enauria looked at Kyle and Airin, in turn. "The last piece of the Crystal won't kill you. I'll make sure of it."

"Good," Airin said.

Enauria cleared her throat. "Jaye is at the Seralyn Capitol Tower."

Kyle sighed in relief.

"So is the Crystal," Enauria said. "Hidden deep underground, inside the Goddess Memorial."

"What is that?" Airin asked.

Enauria looked at the *Seralyn Wave,* hovering in front of them. "It's where you have to go. It's the final resting place for the Goddess Aleria."

"A tomb?" Kyle said. "Beneath the tower?"

"Does anyone know it's there?" Airin asked.

"No one alive knows, not even Fio." Enauria fluffed her hair back. "Think of it as a bank vault for magic. It's underground, but it isn't connected to the tower. It's separate."

"How are we supposed to get there?" Kyle asked.

"Kyle, close your eyes," Enauria said. Kyle hesitated. "It's okay. Close them." After a beat, Kyle shut his eyes. Enauria continued, "I want you to think of the tower. It's a magnificent tree, flourishing in West Scarlet. Uproot the tree, and you'll get to the memorial."

Kyle raised his eyelids. "Are you talking about destroying the Seralyn Capitol Tower?"

"No," Enauria said. "I'm going to tell you how to get to the memorial from the summit of the tower, while I provoke a war."

After being teleported by Enauria, Jaye slouched against the corner of an elevator wall, and his head, cut from shrapnel, drooped. Burns had torn away parts of his shirt and left a gaping tear at his knee. Arlene's death replayed in his mind. Fire devoured and killed her in an instant. He could not say "I'm sorry," bury her, and give her a proper goodbye. The memory of the explosion hid Arlene's face, and when her body was vaporized to spectral ash, Jaye scuttled his back up the wall, panted, and straightened. Her death was real. He did not dream or imagine it.

Plunging waterfalls surrounded the elevator. Clear resin in the ceiling preserved dead butterflies, and maple-colored light beamed through. On the marble floor, the Atrinisy Blade lay next to Jaye's feet. Arlene and Airin had said it had importance, so he picked it up and bobbed it in his hand. The sword was a larger, fancier butterfly knife.

Jaye pulled down a long lever near the exit, and as the doors pulled apart, a breezy mist irritated the cuts on his face. Ahead, a sculpture of unicorns chasing a dragon was centered on a floor of crosscut glass tiles. The largest unicorns were tricolored, black, white, and red. Their depiction had so much ferocity. Jaye carried the Atrinisy Blade outside the elevator and was confronted with a panoramic view of West Scarlet under siege. *What the hell?* Missile batteries and artillery lit the sky, but explosions, jet engines, and midair collisions were silenced. Jaye's eyes went back and forth between the aerial carnage and the sculpture, but the sound of water running underneath distracted him. He approached barrier rails to the side of the elevator and leaned over them to watch how the water supported the platform where he stood in midair. Five stories below, no one was on the main level of the summit.

Jaye staggered toward the sculpture and touched it. The sculpture's hard surface softened the longer he kept his hand in place.

Applying pressure with his fingers shape-shifted the texture from felt to marble to glass. Jaye wondered what type of material constructed the sculpture but knew he would have to research or ask someone to get an answer. He stared upward and backed away from the underside of the sculpture to get a clearer view of the woman who clung to the dragon's wing by impaling it with her sword. Jaye imagined the fury of the sculpture playing out in real life. Wind. Dust. Debris. Scattering everywhere.

A sharp-pitched bell rang from the elevator. Someone approached. Jaye's shoulders tightened because he did not have anywhere to hide. Adrenaline rushed through him, and he ran to the right side of the elevator and raised the Atrinisy Blade in a fighting stance.

The bell rang again. Doors opened, and Arlene's killer emerged from the elevator. If he could not hurt her with a gun, he had to gamble with the sword—payback for Arlene. Enauria's back leg cleared the threshold of the doors, and Jaye rammed the Atrinisy Blade through her, leaving himself wide open for a counterattack.

Enauria wailed as the Atrinisy Blade plunged into her flesh, exiting through her back. She delivered an upward-sweeping diagonal slash and lost her balance, crashing her head against the glass floor. Blood oozed down the left side of her face. She could not scream. The Atrinisy Blade paralyzed the rest of her body and prevented her from using magic.

I have to get this out, she thought, shifting her hand to feel for the sword. The handle was cold and she was too weak to draw the sword out. She needed more time.

Jaye crawled, and his heavy breaths diminished as he approached. He wrenched the Atrinisy Blade from her body, and she gave a twisted cry. The blade rattled as it hit the floor. Jaye lunged for her neck; strangling her through yelps. He straddled and pinned her back to the floor while squeezing harder. Enauria gagged. Writhed. Jammed her hands against Jaye's arms, face, and shoulder blades, waiting for the sword's effect to wear off.

Finally, she thought. A burst of silver lightning repelled Jaye into the air—and stopped time. The silver bolts froze solid and formed a floating grid Enauria used as steps, dashing up them to reach Jaye, upheld in midair, trapped in a revolving slipstream of light. "You can't kill me, not even with the Atrinisy Blade. But I wanted you to try. Kyle told me I shouldn't use people as pawns."

"Then don't."

"We both have our ways, and I was wrong. I'm sorry." Enauria drew her bangs away from her eyes. "I need your help."

"I won't help my fiancée's killer."

Enauria grabbed his wrist, squeezed it, and brought her face close to his. "I didn't kill her. The Crystal did. I'm trying to destroy it, and it's waging a war against me." She let go of Jaye's wrist. "I'll get you to Arlene."

"She's gone."

"Don't you have faith in anything?"

"I do."

"Listen to me." Enauria backed away. "Arlene was pregnant."

Jaye shuddered in horror.

"Arlene never told you because she never knew. If you still have a dream of settling down and being happy, seize it. I can't retrieve the Crystal. I can't use my power against it—but you can. This is the only way to get what you want."

Jaye tried to move but struggled like he was in a straightjacket. "Why are you trying to destroy the Crystal?"

"I'm trying to fix mistakes. Trying to find my happiness." Enauria took a gulp. "The Crystal has three pieces. Help me find the last piece and use it against me. You'll be with Arlene after you complete the job."

The vortex of light around Jaye flared in a paling silver. When the light faded, Jaye had healed from his wounds.

Back inside the cold, deactivated cockpit of the *Delcensia*, he cradled Arlene's engagement ring—returned to him, somehow, by Enauria. The ring should have been gone forever. He pressed his fingertips to it, remembered Arlene, clutched the ring close to his heart, and made the sign of the cross. Enauria promised, and he had hope.

The next day, Jaye was holed up in a one-bed hotel room. It had makeshift beds crafted out of pillows and blankets on the floor, next to duffle bags. The windows were shut and the curtains drawn to block out dust and the sound of road construction in the slums, but tractor pulls and jackhammers could still be heard. Three lamps lit the room, and the area by the table harbored a thick smell of smoke from previous occupants.

Jaye wrote a short list. The United Nations had presumed them MIA and the president would assign Lea-Anne and Katherine to track them down. Jaye hated how he could not contact the Earth or Alerian government, but he enjoyed the challenge of being on the fringe. Enauria requested that their mission be exclusive, and he would abide by her wish.

The Goddess Memorial protected the Seralyn Capitol Tower with a barrier of magic deep underneath the structure. To nullify the barrier, they had to destroy the unicorn sculpture known as *The Advent*, but only the Atrinisy Blade could ensure the sculpture's obliteration. The blade would trigger a release of magic, levitate the tower, and grant access to the memorial from the sky. Simple plan on paper.

Across the table, Kyle twisted his hands together. "Last time we saw Enauria, she said her power was weakening and she wasn't going to teleport us anymore. But she still did it to you."

"I hope that's the last time." Jaye tugged on Arlene's engagement ring, which dangled from his neck on a black chain.

"Why would she take you to the future," Airin said, "to the exact place we're supposed to be—and remove you from there?"

Jaye set his pen down and looked at his gun. "I pawned my watch to get this."

"What?" Airin said.

"Enauria wants us to get there on our own," Kyle said.

"We're out of resources and have less than a week to pull this off." Jaye wrote the word *capital* in the corner of his paper and circled it. "We need money."

"How are we going to get it?" Airin asked.

"We can't touch our emergency accounts," Kyle said. "Or finances of any kind. They're tracked."

Jaye cracked his neck, stood, and holstered his gun. "We'll need comm gear and weapons to infiltrate the Seralyn Capitol Tower." He sat. "Let's be realistic. We might have to boost it."

"Would you feel guilty if you had to steal or get everything by force?" Kyle asked.

"Yes," Jaye said. "But at this point, I'm only concerned about finishing the job. What we want is an edgy score without getting caught."

Jackhammers pounded into the concrete outside.

"Are there alternatives?" Airin asked.

Kyle pressed his lips together, looking at the table. After a few seconds, he raised his head. "Fiona has money."

"Fiona?" Jaye asked.

"Let me see your pen." Kyle took the pen Jaye handed him, opened a pocket notebook, and wrote. "Fiona's supposed to be the next queen of the continent Caneria. She becomes that *in the future*." He tapped the top of the pen against the table. "Right now, Fiona doesn't want to assume the crown because she thinks she isn't ready."

"Where is Fiona?" Airin asked.

"Underground." Kyle grinned. "I have a feeling she's here in West Scarlet."

"We need to find her," Jaye said. "She has access to resources as an heir to the throne and she'll have to be persuaded."

Jaye followed Fiona into a dim jazz lounge called Nocturne. An L-shaped mezzanine jutted into the middle of the venue. It over-looked the stage, where a big band jazz ensemble performed. Jaye sat at a table in the back of the mezzanine and drank a cold burnt-flavored beer. As he worked on the beer, a golden beam flashed out of a rotating light fixture above the stage. The light swayed and pivoted, changing intensity as it cut across the front edge of the mezzanine, shining on Fiona's face.

Fiona sat cross-legged at a table with two couples who were talking loud and laughing. The couples looked like college students or young professionals. The table was littered with glasses of beer and liquor and half-finished appetizer plates. The saxophone player blasted a solo. Fiona shifted her slender body in her seat and tuned out her group's conversation to watch the soloist. Her friends did not notice.

I haven't seen a concert in a long time. Arlene would have enjoyed this, Jaye thought.

The saxophone solo ended, and the band chimed in, one instrument after another, adding layers of sublime harmony. When the band finished its set, Fiona said goodbye to her friends and gave them hugs. She did not stay for the headliner.

Outside of the jazz lounge, Fiona hailed a cab for a ride home. The driver pulled up to the sidewalk, slowing to avoid splashing through rain puddles from a few hours earlier. Fiona went in, and the cab drove away. Jaye lowered the bill of his baseball cap to shield his eyes and flipped the hood of his hooded shirt. He took out his mobile, called Kyle. The cab turned at a stoplight. "She's on the move."

"I'm on her," Kyle said.

. . .

Fiona strolled through an art gallery, passing couples and small groups, keeping to herself. She went to the basement. People drank out of blue plastic cups while others photographed framed art hung in front of a chain-link fence. Cleaning supplies and junk were visible behind the artwork. Several people gathered around Fiona's black-and-white painting called the *Monochrome Nirvana*. Fiona had used an alias on the artist's card affixed next to the work. Attendees discussed her art with a mixed reception, but overall, the opinions pleased her, so she left.

At the third floor, Fiona entered a room surrounded by mirrors and lit by black lights. The exhibit had identical escalators walled off by a layer of glass at each of the room's corners. One pair went up. The other pair, down. One of the four traveled faster than the others, and each of the escalator steps had various designs painted on it: abstract swirls represented galaxies, faces of failed politicians, flags of countries, and extinct animals. The black lights on the ceiling made the designs glow, and patterns from the slow escalators brought back memories of when she had vandalized the walls of her home with paint, as a child.

In a reflection, Kyle came to the doorway. A security guard stopped him because he was holding a drink. Kyle left and returned empty-handed. Fiona circled the exhibit and Kyle met her at the corner of the escalator closest to the exit.

"It's intricate, isn't it?" Kyle said.

Fiona pursed her lips and nodded.

"I drew when I was a kid, but I don't think I could've made anything like this." Fiona walked away, and Kyle asked, "Did I say something wrong?"

She shook her head and went to the hallway.

Kyle hurried without running. "Fiona, I know who you are."

Fiona turned into the stairwell at a brisk pace and gained separation from Kyle, descending the steps.

"I need to talk to you about your mother."

Fiona cleared the stairwell and stopped on the first floor to wait for Kyle. She pointed to the lobby and left the building with him in tow. Outside, live music played, and people lined the street in a nighttime Art Walk. Fiona led Kyle to the side of the art gallery. They were in public view but alone.

Fiona gestured with her hands: *Can you sign?*

Kyle nodded, and they signed the rest of the conversation through the Art Walk's loud music.

Fiona: *What do you know about my mother?*

Kyle: *I'll tell you in a secure location.*

Fiona: *Who are you?*

Kyle: *Kyle Merkailer. I'm with two friends, Jaye DiVista and Airin Asariel. They're waiting in a car.*

Fiona: *Let's go.*

Kyle: *Where?*

Fiona: *Follow me.*

He followed.

Fiona: *If you do anything to jeopardize my cover . . .*

Kyle: *We won't.*

Fiona entered her loft, placed her keys on a mosaic table, and turned on the lights. Stacks of canvases were organized against the wall. Through the windows, brown and orange trees lined an empty, well-lit park across the street. The air conditioner hummed through exposed pipes in the ceiling. Fiona told Jaye to close the door and went to the middle of the loft, keeping her distance from the trio. "How did you find me?"

"Fio," Kyle said, "you and I already know each other."

"No, we don't. And please don't call me Fio."

Kyle looked down, then back at her. "It was Enauria."

"How do you know her?" Fiona asked.

"She's been taking us back and forth through time," Jaye said.

Airin said, "Enauria brought them to my world and told me I had to help them."

"You've been with them ever since?" Fiona asked.

"Ever since," Airin said.

Fiona pointed at Kyle. "And you?"

"You introduced me to Enauria."

"Really?"

"You were Queen of Caneria when we met. She took you from the future and brought you here."

"No," Fiona said in disbelief.

"It's true," Kyle said. "You told me about your mother."

"What did I say about her?" Fiona asked.

"This is verbatim: 'Enauria and I, we're both daughters of the crown. The difference is, I get to continue my mother's legacy.'"

"My mother never returned?"

Kyle shook his head.

"Do you know what happened to her?" Fiona gazed at Kyle.

Kyle hesitated. "She was assassinated . . . in the future."

Fiona sniffled and turned toward the window. "How?"

Jaye said, "Enauria can tell you."

Fiona wiped her eyes, sniffled again, and faced Kyle. "I haven't seen Enauria in years."

"She asked for our help," Kyle said. "To help her, we need yours."

"We'd like you to be our backer," Jaye said.

Fiona looked at Jaye. "When did you last see her?"

"A few days ago."

"Did she tell you I was here?" Fiona asked.

"No," Kyle said. "She didn't tell us anything."

"You're an artist with aliases," Jaye said.

Fiona grinned.

"Will you help us?" Kyle asked.

Fiona said, "My mother's alive right now, but what makes me sad is she'll be lost."

"We can ask Enauria to help you," Jaye said.

Fiona sighed. "I love my mother, but I can only save someone who's worth saving."

"Are you giving up on saving your mother?" Airin asked.

"I never have." Fiona went closer to the three. "Enauria knows the truth about my mother, and if she's in trouble, I have to help her."

Inside her home in Aleria, Enauria watered a lush tree in front of high-walled arching windows and lengthy beige curtains. Her home was a mixture of old styles and modern life that was neither masculine nor feminine. There were dark walls and light accents and preserved plants in black-bordered frames on the walls. Enauria inspected a few of the other live plants in stands by the window, and a high-quality documentary with flashy graphics and a male narrator with deep resonance played in the background.

"In the ancient days, and on another world, the Goddess Aleria fought a sorceress who created a crystal that controlled time. The sorceress used magic to seal herself inside the Crystal to escape death at Aleria's hands. Aleria used the Atrinisy Blade to split the Crystal into five pieces."

Not five. Three, Enauria thought.

"By channeling an overwhelming amount of magic, Aleria almost sacrificed herself as she banished the Crystal shards across the universe so the sorceress would never be resurrected.

"Once the ordeal concluded, Aleria exhausted the remaining energy of her magic and created the planet that bore her name. That new world, forged in the Milky Way galaxy, served as a sanctuary for her recovery."

Enauria placed her watering can on a coffee table, then sat on a long black-and-gold sofa with no pillows.

"Remnants of Aleria's magic produced Trees of the Edystar—tall, luxuriant trees that glowed when swept by the wind. The Great Trees gave birth to the first Alerian people, known as Children of the Edystar—the goddess's descendants, which brought human life to the realm.

"The Great Trees are now extinct, but smaller Edystar trees exist on Aleria. As time passed from the ancient days to the present, magic within the trees dissipated."

The Edystar tree at Ceremony Falls is my favorite, she thought.

The narrator continued. "Queen Caneria was a member of a royal lineage that made up the descendants of the last Great Tree. Caneria had said that the first Edystar children had memories of Aleria through magic. These memories were idealized projections of how Aleria saw herself in the future. Aleria desired to be a strong, intelligent, confident woman—but sometime after the goddess was rescued from the Olihoricon Tower hundreds of years ago, she departed and was never seen again."

Enauria *tsk*ed. She got up and walked to the opposite side of the room to practice shooting pool on a table near another window. A chill ran through her body. Two centuries ago, she'd found the Goddess Aleria dead in a hotel room, engulfed in a nebula of magic. Years before her death, Aleria's face was framed by dark, curling locks. People gravitated toward her amber eyes, eyes Enauria regretted, and sometimes wished she could have gouged out. Part of Enauria hated Aleria for creating the world but not contributing to its development. The citizens of her planet believed in the goddess, despite her reclusiveness. When Enauria was a teenager, she wondered how her ancestors and people across the world had formed religions, devotions, and likenesses of a woman they had never seen. They prayed to her, for her. And with the world open to the interstellar community, they prayed to God, other gods, multiple deities, or no one. The unforgettable nebula, colored green, white, and gold, engulfing Aleria's body never went away. Even goddesses could commit suicide. Enauria never knew how or why it happened, so she blamed a mental disorder.

Enauria abandoned her cue, ignored several late bills addressed to her alias, and sat in an arced recliner. On the living room wall, a chalkboard documented the history of how the Crystal had become part of her life. She retraced the steps in her head: The Goddess Aleria had slept at the Olihoricon Tower, and an expedition to awaken and kidnap Aleria for her powers was launched. Enauria prevented that plan and rescued Aleria with her cousin Fherazin.

Battling terrorists and falling from the tower changed her life. She never forgot screaming as she tumbled through the air, powerless, even with her training and magic. The fall should have killed her, but before she slammed into the ground, a blue light in midplunge made her blank out.

Enauria woke to find Caneria and the Goddess Aleria standing by her bedside. At the time, Aleria looked like a high school student, far from what the statues and paintings glorified her to be. The goddess had told her that Pearl Light had saved her life, but years later, she learned the spirit-energy Pearl Light inhabited her body, allowing her to control time.

Pearl Light never possessed Enauria. It had no voice, never tried to communicate with her, and respected her free will. Pearl Light was a parasite spirit content with thriving on her emotions.

Enauria spent years learning what Pearl Light could do. She self-studied, discovering new abilities: teleportation, telepathy, manipulating time, traveling through it, and shifting herself between dimensions. On many occasions, Enauria injured herself, caused accidents, endured trial and error. When she mastered her abilities, a superiority complex ensued, and she left Aleria to test the threshold of her powers.

Centuries passed, but time flowed different for Enauria. Physically she had aged less than fifteen years, but her mental health suffered. She had been the universe's most privileged tourist, but she'd become obsessed with experimenting with Pearl Light. She'd forgotten about her own life, aspirations, and happiness. Enauria returned to West Scarlet—in the future, battling depression. She visited a psychiatrist, reconnected with Fiona, and, out of compassion, helped Fiona, at her request, to find and rescue Caneria from exile.

In the future, after a short return home, coordinated suicide bombers and joint missile strikes killed Caneria inside Castle

Ascaria with the element of surprise. The blasts caused instant death. Caneria was a skilled magic user but had no way to protect herself. The antimonarchy insurgency claimed responsibility for the attack.

Caneria's assassination sent Enauria further into emotional turmoil. She had lost her closest friend, the last person besides Fiona whom she could call family. Sometime after Caneria was killed, Enauria escaped an assassination attempt. She promised Fiona she would hunt and kill everyone responsible for her mother's death.

The Crystal had been divided into three pieces. Enauria discovered where the pieces were by crusading through time to research. What surprised her the most was finding out Pearl Light was the third piece of the Crystal—and the Centerpiece Affair, a campaign launched hundreds of years ago on Aleria to find the Crystal, was active and responsible for Queen Caneria's death. That plan would not stop until the Crystal was obtained.

Enauria knew her mission: destroy the Crystal responsible for her heartache and purge Pearl Light from her body. She wanted to settle down, embrace happiness and peace. A problem ensued. Pearl Light became aware and took measures to stop her. Pearl Light made sure Enauria could not be killed and did not allow her to harm herself with magic or any weapon she wielded.

Enauria planned to take the Atrinisy Blade and the Crystal and have others complete the job for her. She rose from the chair, straightened dead tree branches in a turquoise vase, and walked to reclaim her cue.

Jaye rushed through an empty corridor, following a chain of lights that reflected over a polished floor. At the end of the hall, he opened a sliding door. The *Delcensia* was crammed into storage like a motorcycle squeezed between two parked cars. Lea-Anne stood by the left wall, holding a suppressed gun parallel to her leg. Jaye was not surprised. Being tracked by Lea-Anne was a testament to her skills. She knew some of the *Delcensia*'s specs. The plane had to be secure, hidden from people, but close enough to access. Lea-Anne required no effort to break into a civilian-run storage facility.

"You disappeared from Sel Tresel. President ordered me to find you, and we did, thanks to this." Lea-Anne looked at the *Delcensia*. "Why haven't you reported?"

"Arlene was kidnapped a week ago."

"How?"

"She was hit by an IED and taken away."

"Any casualties?"

Jaye shook his head. "I've been off-grid because Enauria's helping me track the kidnapper."

She frowned. "You've defected?"

"I haven't defected." Jaye approached a metal chest underneath the *Delcensia*.

"I have to report this," Lea-Anne said. "You'll lose your job."

"I'm trying to save Arlene."

"With Enauria?"

"If I don't get airborne, I'll never get her back. Are you gonna let that happen?"

Lea-Anne unscrewed the silencer and put the gun back in her purse. "Let me help you. Infinity's in West Scarlet."

Jaye smirked. "Thanks, but I have to do this by myself."

"You don't have to."

"I do."

"Katherine and I can—"

"No." Jaye checked his watch. "Report to the president. Tell him you weren't able to find me."

"I'm not doing that."

Jaye knelt and opened the matte black chest. Flight gear and supplies were inside. He fished through the chest, retrieved a brand-new pack of playing cards, and handed them to Lea-Anne. "Give this to him and tell him he has all the aces he'll ever need."

Airin struck the foundation of the unicorn sculpture inside the Seralyn Capitol Tower with repeated blows. Breaks appeared and he kept swinging. The back of one unicorn shattered, but several had to be destroyed to collapse the statue. Antipersonnel mines exploded at the base of the room. Soldiers wailed and reinforcements secured the atrium floor. Three minutes. Bringing down the statue with the sword was impossible. The blade was too thin and he needed more time.

Bullets chipped the glass deck. Sharpshooters. Airin climbed the unicorns and zigzagged through constant gunfire. A group of soldiers triggered another set of planted explosives, destroying the elevator shaft and the staircase wrapped around it. Airin held on as the upper deck rocked. Sniper rounds resumed, shredding through the glass, missing his body. Airin squeezed through a gap between unicorns and climbed the sculpture from its inner axis. The waterfalls stopped.

"They're changing tactics," Airin said.

Soldiers' voices echoed without the waterfalls, but he could not make out what they said. Airin emerged and took refuge on the back of the dragon atop the sculpture—its spread wings prevented him from being seen. A five-story gap separated Airin from the soldiers on the atrium floor. He conjured the Atrinisy Blade and hacked the neck of the dragon. The head tumbled and crashed onto the glass, drawing fracture lines across the deck.

Tear gas canisters launched and fell near the sculpture's base. Two more waves of tear gas followed. The canisters amassed and the smoke expanded. Another canister landed next to him, followed by a hiss as the gas diffused. Airin coughed, kicked the canister away, dismissed the Atrinisy Blade, and swung to a unicorn below the dragon. He held his breath and braced himself as another tremor hit. Hydraulics retracted the platform supporting the sculpture back to the atrium floor.

Airin re-summoned the Atrinisy Blade and sliced underneath the dragon, causing it to collapse and fall through the glass. A round tore through Airin's vest and his upper left shoulder. He lost his balance, dropped the Atrinisy Blade, and fell, breaking his fall over the back of a unicorn while holding onto its crest with one hand. The Atrinisy Blade plummeted to the deck, but Airin made it disappear. He pulled himself back onto the unicorn, grimaced from the pain of the bullet wound and the toxicity of the air, and rearmed the sword. Blood flowed from his wound as the deck continued to retract. He wondered how many soldiers assembled, which position he would attack first, and if he would have to kill all of them to save his own life.

A flash of light made Airin shield his face, and he hunkered as a jet stream threw soldiers and spilled glass from the windows. Airin winced as pieces gashed the back of his head. Jet engines and explosions outside the Seralyn Capitol Tower filled the room. Airin covered his ears as the *Delcensia,* fresh from its wake, hovered and strafed the atrium floor with its Gatling-style cannons.

Jaye released his finger from the *Delcensia*'s trigger, and the cannon rotors whirled to a stop. The controls shuddered as the glass platform pushed on the *Delcensia*. Jaye reversed the plane, clearing the cockpit and tail stabilizers from being crushed, and wedged the aircraft against the glass deck to prevent the platform from lowering farther. He set the autopilot, opened the canopy, jumped onto the glass, and climbed *The Advent*.

"I'm getting you out of here." Jaye took out a shot of morphine from a sleeve in his flight suit and injected it into Airin's arm.

Airin sighed and looked at the rest of the sculpture. "It's not done."

"I'll finish it."

Airin gave Jaye the Atrinisy Blade. Jaye stepped to a ledge on Airin's side, planted his right foot back, and grunted as he hacked. He did not have the arm strength to keep this up. Backup forces unleashed machine-gun fire from the main floor. Bullets pounded the underside of the *Delcensia*. There was no time to destroy the sculpture with the Atrinisy Blade and save the plane. "I'm going to use the *Delcensia* to bring down the sculpture. Get on the back and hang on."

Airin grimaced a hard yes and braced himself. Jaye scrambled back to the *Delcensia*, wishing it seated two. He stashed the Atrinisy Blade behind the pilot's seat, shut the canopy, and strapped himself in. The *Delcensia* lifted, imploding the glass, and piggybacked *The Advent* as it separated from the platform.

A rocket-propelled grenade struck the *Delcensia* and gave Jaye whiplash as he prepared to reopen the canopy. Damage indicators flashed and alarms rang, but Jaye ignored them to maintain control of the plane. He unleashed another volley of cannon fire in the direction the RPG came from. If he was lucky, no one would have the guts to retrieve the missile launcher for another round. The smell of black smoke crept into the cockpit, and Jaye turned on an external camera.

On the screen, the sculpture was still piggybacked. Airin fell onto the top side of the plane, slid to the port tail stabilizer, and grabbed hold. Airin signaled to go, but Jaye did not wake the *Delcensia* with Airin outside. He had to get clear of the combat zone. Before any surviving soldiers counterattacked, Jaye kicked in the vertical afterburners, which propelled the *Delcensia* and *The Advent* out of the tower.

Airin shouted as the *Delcensia*'s velocity changed. He tightened his grip on the tail stabilizer and held on for dear life. The plane shot straight up, and the afterburners deafened him. His body swung and he fought to straighten himself and not get thrown off. The cold air numbed his hands, and the high speed placed crushing pressure on Airin. He thought his bullet wound would tear and cleave his body, and he wished he had a harness or a parachute. Ships and planes engaged in battle above West Scarlet, and anti-aircraft batteries shelled the sky. Clasping onto the *Delcensia* for an entire flight would be impossible. *I'm going to die*, Airin thought.

The sculpture fell parallel to the tower and Jaye fired a missile to obliterate it in midair. He grinned at the explosion and was pleased he saved his passenger's life, but an alarm ruined the ideal opportunity to escape. The *Delcensia* was in missile lock. Close proximity. Jaye released countermeasures, and the missile blew up. There was a shockwave, another missile warning, and eleven o'clock crossfire. Jaye did not want Airin to be shredded by cannon fire, so he jabbed the stick, punched the throttle, and blasted away from the tower.

Airin screamed—jettisoned from the *Delcensia*—snatching air with his hands as he tried to catch the plane in desperation, but it drew out of reach. Parachute training came back to Airin. He turned his body into a proper dive, closed his eyes. Embers from the sculpture whipped his face. Some legacy.

Jaye cursed and backtracked, hoping to find Airin in free fall, when a distracting halo encircled the tower and vanished. Airin was gone, and Jaye cursed more. He wished he had another way to save Airin instead of carrying him on top of the aircraft. He wanted to hunt for the plane or drone that launched the missile at him, but there were too many, and they belonged to West Scarlet's military, which he was not fighting. Jaye raged inside the cockpit, then stopped. He could not allow the burden of loss and his emotions to best him. If he did not get away now, he would be killed in combat. Jaye slowed his breathing, turned on the radio, and declared an emergency. He programmed a wake, and the *Delcensia* disappeared in a flash of blue light.

Five minutes later, Jaye shoved open the bathroom door, went to the sink, ran his hands underneath the faucet, and splashed water on his face. He bridged his hand over his forehead, groaned in frustration. He looked up into the mirror at Kyle, who had followed him. Jaye unzipped the top of his flight suit.

"It's not your fault," Kyle said. "You did what you could."

Jaye slammed the rim of the sink and kicked the wall. "I tried to save Airin, not get him killed!"

Fiona approached from the hallway and handed a towel to Jaye. "I'm sorry."

Jaye took the towel and wiped his face. "We were supposed to destroy the sculpture with *only* the Atrinisy Blade." He snickered. "I used a missile on it!"

Fiona said, "That's why the tower didn't rise."

"But we saw the light," Kyle said, "so something must've gone right."

"We have to fix this." Jaye stormed out of the bathroom.

In the kitchen, Jaye peeked through an opening in the wall. The *Delcensia* was in the living room of Fiona's townhouse. It had smashed through walls and crushed furniture post-wake. Jaye marveled at how the plane did not collapse the place. He faced Kyle and Fiona. Kyle studied blueprints of the tower from computer screens, glancing, on occasion, at a live feed of the battle outside.

Nearby, Fiona watched the news. The newscast header read, "Syndicate and Nonpareil Strike Forces Attack West Scarlet." A reporter delivered an update, but Jaye did not listen because he had an idea. "I can wake the *Delcensia* into the memorial."

Kyle turned his head. "Absolutely not."

"It's our only play."

"You can get yourself killed."

"We don't have options," Jaye said.

"Give me more time."

"The memorial isn't in the blueprints."

Kyle stood. "You can't blind wake a plane. Ever." He pointed to the living room. "Look at this! You won't be as lucky if you don't know your location."

Jaye would have pulled rank with Lea-Anne, but with Kyle, the situation was different. The chain of command had become a democracy now, which Jaye accepted because he needed Kyle's help to survive.

Fiona's shoulders drooped while watching images of the battle flood the news. Her heartbeat slowed and her thoughts focused on the injured and killed citizens, the property destroyed in the city. Concern for political and military leaders followed. What would they do? For the first time in centuries, Fiona was in a city she loved, caught in the mayhem of war, unable to do anything. But in reality, she had an avenue to power. Fiona realized her strong desire to help and wanted to act on it. She was ready to become queen.

Enauria's voice spoke through telepathy: *Fio, I'm here.*

Fiona closed her eyes. *After so many years*, she thought, *why are you reaching out to me now?*

In deep focus, Fiona felt the aura of Enauria: a sensation of flames, wrapped in the magic of the Goddess Memorial. She opened her eyes. Enauria had shown her how to find the Goddess Memorial.

Fiona cut between Jaye and Kyle. "The magic protecting the memorial is gone, but it's still underground." She looked back at the live feed of the battle. "My city is getting ruined and people are dying when they shouldn't."

Jaye glanced at the *Delcensia*.

"It's too risky," Kyle said.

"Kyle's right," Fiona said. "You can't teleport the plane without knowing where you're supposed to go. I'll take both of you to Enauria since she's there."

"You can teleport?" Jaye asked. "That's convenient."

"I can, but it comes with a price. I lose years of my life. It could be five, a hundred, or half. I'll never know. That's why I avoid the spell. I hate the consequences, but that's the price of learning this magic. Enauria can teleport without side effects, and I used to be jealous, but I'm not anymore because she has other burdens." Fiona paused. "Get your things ready."

Within the hour, Fiona sensed for the memorial from the townhouse. The Seralyn Capitol Tower had never given off a trace of magical energy its entire life. With the destruction of *The Advent,* Fiona felt magic that was not there, but only when she closed her eyes and concentrated on it. Fiona chose where to teleport based on feeling the memorial's magic, its intensity—and the presence of space. The memorial felt like heat from a firestorm. Fiona drew herself closer to the mental sensation of the flames. If she moved farther away, the sensation dulled. Fiona sensed for a constant and steady flame, and when she found it, she willed herself to teleport Kyle and Jaye, who brought the Atrinisy Blade, with her. They vanished from the townhouse and reappeared in the sand.

The Goddess Memorial was a cathedral nave with a vaulted ceiling. There were no chairs, decorations, or windows, but light created from magic shined into the room from recesses in the walls. A landslide barricaded the entrance doors, and time had damaged the memorial's dusty-gray walls. Sand covered the floor, and an ornate chain of elevated, corroded-bronze walkways zigzagged to the altar, where Enauria waited.

Fiona's ears tingled from the cold. She genuflected, closed her eyes, and placed the thumb and middle finger of her left hand to her temples. The east lights flickered. "I can't get us out. The magic around the memorial resealed."

Kyle said, "We're locked in."

"Try again," Jaye said.

Fiona sighed. "It won't work."

The east lights weakened a notch.

"What's going on with the light?" Kyle asked.

"It's getting dimmer. Enauria will take care of this, so let's get her the Crystal." Jaye raised the Atrinisy Blade, placed it on the walkway, scaled the passage rails, and picked up the sword.

Kyle followed Jaye onto the walkway and offered Fiona help, but she shook her head and grabbed onto the bridge. Fiona's arms strained as she pulled herself up, so she boosted herself with her feet to make up for a lack of upper-body strength. She went over the rail and kicked the sand off her shoes. Jaye led the way across the corroded path, eager in step but careful. He gained confidence in his stride because the bridge was not rickety. Enauria watched their approach. They reached the end of the pathway, and Fiona wanted to hug her at the altar.

"Don't come closer," Enauria said.

Fiona stopped and narrowed her gaze. "Enauria, what

happened to my mother? Where is she? They said she gets assassi-nated in the future."

"Fio . . ."

"You lure me here and can't even tell me?"

The south lights dwindled.

"Because it changes nothing." Enauria looked at Jaye. "The Crystal is here on the altar."

"No, not yet." Fiona stretched her arm to barricade Jaye.

"I'm sorry, Fio, but this isn't about you right now."

All light from the east wall went out.

"I won't let them give you the Crystal until I find out."

"Fio, you were never supposed to find her."

Fiona quivered. "How can you say that?" Half the memorial became dark.

Enauria softened her tone. "I didn't. Your mother did."

Fiona did not speak.

"In the future," Enauria said, "we rescued your mother. She went from exiled to assassinated. For what?"

The north wall by the altar faded.

Enauria continued: "You ran away from the crown out of love for her, but it's your responsibility now."

"I know," Fiona said. "I'm ready to take the crown, but before I do, I need to know how she died."

"I can't tell you."

Fiona stepped forward. "I need closure."

The entire memorial became dark.

Enauria drew her sword and dissolved it into a flux of blue light that lit the space between them. "Kyle, the Crystal is on this altar. I want you to get it and—"

Fiona blocked Kyle. "Don't even try." She shot a look at Jaye. "You, too."

"I need them, Fio. We'll never get out of here if you don't let them help me."

"Tell me what happened."

Enauria raised her sword and guided the light over Fiona's face. Caneria would have been proud of Fio's restored path to the crown. "The Crystal caused your mother's exile, and it should be destroyed."

"You can't save her?"

"Not from dying. I tried, and when I did, I felt like I was being burned alive. I'd collapse, get teleported to another time—and the flames stayed with me like phantom pains and lingered for hours, days, even weeks. Any further and I would've died. It hurts when I think of your mother. I don't want to die. I want to live. That's what this is about. You have a future ahead of you, and I want mine too." Enauria pointed her sword toward the altar and the emanating light swayed with her momentum.

Fiona said, "I'm sorry," but Enauria did not expect an apology. She thought Fiona would have asked more questions about her mother's death. Accepting the death of a loved one was difficult. Enauria regretted lacking the knowledge of how her mother died. She wanted to travel back to find out if her mother was ill, assassinated, or had died in peace. Did she die brokenhearted? Uncertainty left a scar in Enauria's soul. She defied her by not accepting the arranged marriage, leaving home—only to return to a dead mother she could not save. Pearl Light had locked Enauria from revisiting and changing important moments in her life, and it had driven her crazy until she'd learned to accept it.

"Let me do this for you," Fiona said.

"I'd be honored," Enauria said.

Fiona walked to the altar, and Jaye said, "I thought you wanted us to do that."

"You will," Enauria said. "Let Fio give it to you."

With delicate handling, Fiona retrieved the silvery-blue Crystal from a circular recess in the altar's center. The Crystal had hairline fractures across its base. Enauria's heart beat quicker in anticipation. The end of her journey was near.

Fiona presented the Crystal, but Enauria kept her hands away. "What's wrong?"

"Nothing." Enauria wrapped a hand around Fiona's wrist. "Hold the Crystal tight and give it to Kyle."

The Crystal pulsed as the exchange took place.

The Crystal flashed a soft white light and Jaye feared Kyle would die the same way Arlene had. He readied the Atrinisy Blade to strike Enauria.

Kyle locked the Crystal in his hand. He wanted to feel good instead of nervous, and he liked how Enauria calmed herself with a Zen-like stillness. The light from the Crystal ebbed as Kyle thought about relaxing in a chair, underneath a tree in the late afternoon. He imagined reading a book, stopping to watch slow-moving clouds against a purplish, pinkish sky. Between pages, he would sip a margarita, and when the sun went down, he would go inside, watch a movie, and take a long, warm bath. Kyle thought about sex with Fiona, how he made too much money without being able to enjoy it, and that he could die at any moment. He dreamed about marrying Fiona and raising a child. The idea made him smile even if it would never happen. *No regrets,* he thought.

"I have to do one last thing. The memorial shouldn't be in darkness." Enauria charged a vortex of silver lightning near her hand. The lightning sounded like an erratic generator building pressure. She turned away from Jaye and Kyle, threw her sword to the floor, pitched the lightning to the sword like a baseball slider, and the lightning devoured the sword. A hand gesture catapulted the sword into the air and destroyed it. The metal's shapeshifting light magic released particles in the air and gave permanent light to the Goddess Memorial.

Blue stars scattered across the memorial and reminded Jaye of suspended fireworks. When he was growing up, he celebrated Fourth of July with family. Memories of the past bridged to daydreams of life with Arlene and two children. A boy would tug on his leg and cheer at the biggest explosion. A daughter, propped on his shoulder, would eat a melting ice cream cone, while Arlene stood next to him and wrapped her arm around his waist. Bursts of colorful fireworks made the family smile. The dream would be real if Enauria fulfilled her promise.

"Jaye." Enauria stood straight, as if she were ready for her own execution. "Do it."

He tightened his grip on the Atrinisy Blade but hesitated. At the Seralyn Capitol Tower, he had attacked her point-blank—and she'd survived. Intuition told him he would kill her this time. If she died, how would he get Arlene back? Enauria closed her eyes and placed her hands behind her back. Jaye's heart beat faster, and his hands and forehead sweated.

"Do it!" Enauria said in a more aggressive tone.

Jaye clenched his teeth. He transferred the Atrinisy Blade to his left hand, wiped the sweat from his palm, took the sword back into his right hand, and secured his grip a final time.

Enauria opened her eyes and glared at him. "Come on, Jaye!"

She squeezed her hands behind her back and pressed her thumbs, hard. She anticipated Jaye's attack. The Atrinisy Blade would disable her magic, leaving her with enough time to cast one spell. She relaxed her hands, shifted her thumbs, kept her head and body straight, and glanced at Fiona.

Kyle frowned. Why'd she look at Fiona?

Jaye imagined waking up next to Arlene in bed. She smiled at him, kissed him, and whispered good morning. They lived in peace. No more running. No more killing. "You'll be with Arlene," Enauria had said. Jaye believed Enauria, and he did not believe her. Arlene was dead. How was he supposed to see her again? More than anything, he needed fury. Enauria had robbed him of his future and unborn child, if that story were true. He screamed and lunged forward at breakneck speed, ramming the Atrinisy Blade into Enauria.

Enauria gasped, clutching her chest after the blade plowed through her. Breathing quickened. An intense high surged through her, followed by an extreme crash. The ability to use magic drained fast from her body.

Kyle knew the sheer force Jaye had used to shove the blade into Enauria's flesh would deck her. He launched himself at full speed to intercept Enauria while she stumbled backward.

Jaye let go of the Atrinisy Blade when he could not press it past Enauria's rib cage. He forced himself to a complete stop, and as he separated from Enauria, Kyle bolted in front of him and uppercut the underside of Enauria's jaw, jerking her head sideways.

Enauria concentrated through the pain and teleported Fiona out of the Goddess Memorial.

The Crystal triggered a shock wave, blowing everyone in the room back, killing Jaye and Kyle. Their bodies landed in the coarse sand below the corroded-bronze walkways.

Fiona experienced vertigo. Her body smashed into the *Delcensia,* breaking the cockpit window. She fell to the floor of her townhouse, landed on her back, rolled to her side, and lay still.

Enauria screamed as the shock wave triggered a magical exorcism. An inferno of blue light engulfed her as she sailed through the air. She dropped onto the walkway leading to the altar, tumbled off its edge, and fell sideways into the sand with splayed arms and legs. Blood was everywhere. Coldness overtook Enauria, and her body trembled. A moment later, she kicked sand, writhed, and fought through incinerating pain. Spasms contorted her face. She spit blood and saliva and sand until her mouth dried.

Pain increased. Enauria dug her hands and arms into the sand, closed her eyes, and tightened her hands to grab fistfuls of sand. An aura around her body exploded into a fierce lightning storm. Enauria gave an exasperated sigh, and the blazing sensation ended.

When she opened her eyes, a crater had formed around her, charring the sand. She blinked, kept still, and heard herself breathing. Everything else was silent. She shifted her hands out of the sand, pulled the Atrinisy Blade, and screamed while removing the sword from her body. Free of the weapon, she panted and discarded the bloodstained metal. Enauria touched the gaping wound caused by the sword. She winced, pulled her fingers away, and rubbed the warm blood on her fingertips—thinking of curative magic.

Magic returned, but she did not heal right away. Instead, Enauria relished the thin line between life and death, keeping her eyes on the blue stars shining underneath the ceiling. The stars motivated her to leave the memorial to see real stars.

Disgusted by blood, Enauria healed herself with magic and stood once her wounds disappeared. The skin where the Atrinisy Blade had pierced bore no scar. She ran her hands along the length of her arms, rotated her shoulder blades, and cracked her neck. Without Pearl Light, she was liberated. She gave a short sigh, bent a knee and picked up the Atrinisy Blade. The blackened sand by her feet made her remember Jaye and Kyle, whose bodies she still had to locate. Their sacrifice would not be in vain.

Enauria raised her hand. Three dominant lines in her palm were scars from training as a child. She wondered if she could still cast silver bolts of lightning—and took the longest breath of her life. "Is Pearl Light gone?"

Fiona woke up startled by broken glass, which shifted underneath her body. Soreness in her back caused her to stand slowly, and she ignored the small cuts and scrapes along her arms. She called Enauria's name, but there was no answer. Kyle's and Jaye's names were next. The silence was unnerving. "I'm alone." Fiona brushed off any clinging pieces of glass, tugged on her blouse to make it snug, and shook her head in disbelief. The house was a wreck. A fighter jet had crashed into her living room—an impromptu art piece Fiona considered preserving.

Smoke from the battle lingered in the air, accompanying the setting sun. Fiona stepped over debris and went near the windows. No more explosions; a different silence to enjoy. She ran her hands through her hair to smooth it, looked back at the *Delcensia*, and thought about Jaye's argument with Kyle—waking the plane to get to the memorial. She closed her eyes and concentrated on returning to the memorial, but the energy of flame she had sensed earlier had ceased.

By the wall, a vintage record player was on a tabletop stand. Fiona went to the turntable, started the platter, and lowered the needle onto the grooves of a record. A piano sonata filled the room. Fiona raised the volume and thought about going outside, but stayed indoors to admire the light out the window. For everyone who died, she would make a difference rebuilding West Scarlet, and herself.

Aperture 52

Enauria always celebrated the death anniversaries of people who meant the most to her. She stargazed underneath a time-chiseled tree near the peak of Aleria's tallest waterfall. The evergreen held an aroma of pine, and the spicy-honey scent of its bark mixed with freshwater mist in the nighttime air. Ceremony Falls had a serene and constant heavy plunge. Wind fluttered Enauria's hair and ruffled the crisp broad-leaves, which glowed like a field of fireflies with each breeze. Once the wind settled, shards of gemlike dust fell from the tree onto Enauria and sprinkled the surrounding ground.

Enauria took her hands out of her insulated jacket pockets and waved her right hand across an empty lantern, charging it with a bright, steady flame. The flame revealed two granite gravestones: Jaye DiVista and Arlene Asariel, side by side. Between them was an unopened bottle of red wine. She lit a second lantern by the gravestones of Kyle Merkailer and Airin Asariel. The four graves made a square. Airin had a one hundred forty-year-old bottle of wine over his grave. Kyle's gift was a Gibraltar glass filled with coffee beans.

In solitude with light and dark and nature, Enauria listened to the waterfalls, planning her next move.

Finis.

Acknowledgments

Mom and Dad: Thank you for your unwavering love and support. If it wasn't for your combined efforts, I wouldn't be who I am today. You gave me the resources to pursue writing growing up. Without your positive influence, none of this would've been possible.

To my professors when I was at UC Riverside Palm Desert: Tod Goldberg, thanks for accepting me into a stellar MFA program. It transformed the way I read and write. Elizabeth Crane, Rob Roberge, and Mark Haskell Smith: Your guidance showed me what literary writing is. Jill Alexander Essbaum and Matthew Zapruder: Your poetry classes gave me crossover ideas I fused into my genre fiction. To my UCR classmates, your comments and our talks at residency improved details and helped me add things I missed. The work is stronger because of your contributions.

Alex Chow, my cover illustrator: When I saw your artwork online, I knew you were the right person to design the *Reflections of Destiny* art. You depicted Enauria with grace and brought to life a scene I imagined in my mind for years. It's wonderful and ethereal. Thanks for taking on the commission.

To my editor, Sandra N. Smith: You brought an impressive punch and conciseness to this novella that would've been lost without your editing prowess. Thanks for corresponding and getting to know the work with me. Copy-and-pasted sentences and misspelled acronyms can be ninjas lurking in paragraphs that only fresh eyes can discover.

Ryan R. Reyna: You were one of my earliest readers, and always a supporter. With your experience in graphic design, it's fitting you added the finishing touches to the book by designing an awesome cover. I'm glad the inspiration struck you when it did.

One of my best and oldest friends, Abraham C. Lleva: You're a storyteller whose writing has always motivated me. I'm honored that you've seen every major draft of this project since high school. Sharing the story with you and getting your feedback has been invaluable and instrumental in helping me revise. You understood my inspirations, ideas, and characters—and your critiques allowed me to write those things in a way that made sense.

Maryfaith Barbin: My lovely and amazing wife. For one of my birthdays, you learned do-it-yourself bookbinding, and surprised me with a hardcover copy of *Reflections of Destiny*. What a fantastic keepsake. That gift motivated me to complete this project. Thanks for helping me to look inward to better understand my characters by imagining what they think and feel. At first, I focused on style and action. What the reader could see. You challenged me to develop my characters. I added pieces here and there, but it wasn't until later that it clicked. You've helped me with improving details, adjusting lines of dialogue, quality checking scenes, and getting me through moments of indecision I had with the text. You enabled me to focus and revise. Without that, this novella would be a digital paperweight. Thank you for being my constant, and steering me toward my dream of publication. I love you!

To my readers: The world is full of art. Thanks for taking the time to read mine. I hope you enjoy the story.

About the Author

Benzon Ray Barbin is a writer + photographer + hi-fi enthusiast who has loved science fiction and fantasy since he was a kid. He has an MFA in Creative Writing from the University of California, Riverside. San Diego, California, is home, where Benn loves coffee dates with his beautiful wife, Maryfaith.